PENNY OATES

SWAN
PRINCESS

Complete and Unabridged

LINFORD
Leicester

First published in Great Britain in 2019

First Linford Edition
published 2020

A catalogue record for this book is available
from the British Library.

ISBN 978–1–4448–4616–4

Published by
Ulverscroft Limited
Anstey, Leicestershire

Set by Words & Graphics Ltd.
Anstey, Leicestershire
Printed and bound in Great Britain by
T. J. International Ltd., Padstow, Cornwall

This book is printed on acid-free paper

SWAN PRINCESS

Talented young ballerina Gina is struggling following the death of her mother, the failure of her choreographer father's new ballet, and the desertion of her fiancé, David. Trying to support her grieving father and save the ballet company her parents set up, she is outraged when rich, brooding businessman Jude Alexander criticises her approach and offers to become a partner. His money could solve all their problems — but she suspects his motives, and vows to fight him tooth and nail . . .

1

'I have to say, Miss George, it really is a very generous offer, and owing to the parlous state of the company's finances, one which I feel I must urge you to consider most seriously.'

Paul Lindt fiddled with his tie, uncomfortable under the direct gaze of the slender girl sitting opposite him. As bank manager to the Eastern Ballet he knew his advice was sound, but he feared it would not be taken. He was right.

'No!' Georgina George shook her head vehemently, and audiences used to the unbearable poignancy of her huge doe-like eyes would have been understandably taken aback had they seen the warning glint they held.

The banker sighed and spread his hands expressively as if about to speak.

'No,' repeated Gina, more quietly but

with no less emphasis, 'we don't want some wretched grocer telling us what to do.'

'Jude Alexander is hardly a grocer!' Mr Lindt was shocked to hear so important a businessman thus described. 'He did start off with supermarkets, it's true, but his company, Relly Holdings, has diversified into many different fields since then.'

'Ballet?' she demanded.

'Er, no — but he's eager to try a new sphere — '

'Well, we're not eager to be the company he practises on!'

Gina looked so slight and pliable that it was often difficult for others to remember that in reality she had muscles of steel, honed by a lifetime of physically exacting ballet classes. Her will was equally unyielding, and Paul Lindt accepted that anything further he might say could only worsen the situation.

'Very well. I shall tell him you are not interested at this time.'

'Not just at this time, not ever!'

The bank manager tried one last tack.

'My dear, do consider your position. The wonderful summer last year meant box office receipts were down, the première of *Anna Karenina* was hardly a success, and what with David Bryant leaving the company . . . ' He remembered too late and broke off.

'Yes, thank you, Mr Lindt, I know.'

It was strange how the mere mention of his name could hurt her still. She was over him, of course — it was eighteen months since he left. Yet in spite of being able to accept that he had never really loved her, and had simply used her, others speaking of him could still cause her pain.

Mr Lindt was pink with embarrassment. How could he have been so insensitive? The newspapers had been full of the story at the time. *Premier Danseur leaves financée to star in America.* He stood up, gathering his papers. Truth to tell, he never felt totally at ease with these theatre types.

'Goodbye.' Gina extended her hand, and as he returned her dazzling smile, he thought what a damn fool David Bryant must have been to leave behind such a beautiful creature.

* * *

Gina watched him go. She felt sorry for the fussy little man, suspecting, rightly, that he was one of the old school who was not comfortable with women in positions of authority, and only turned to her because her father was so vague.

And he *was* vague. James George, choreographer and founder of the Eastern Ballet — a genius, critics said. Where his artistic direction was concerned, she agreed, but as for everyday life? She flung up her hands in despair.

The trouble was, although she had a more practical brain and did her best to understand the accounts she pored over for hours on end, she was the first to admit she was no businesswoman herself. The bank manager was right, they needed a financial director and administrator — but after David, she doubted she would ever again put a man in any position of trust within the company.

'Paul gone?'

James George popped his head around the office door, his signature silver cigarette holder in hand. Ever since the smoke-free legislation came in years ago, he'd wandered around public buildings with a pristine sobranie filter in place, just waiting for the moment he could escape outside and light up.

'Yes, you timed that very well.'

His gaunt, expressive face creased with laughter. 'You know how much I hate talking business. What did he say?'

'Pretty much what he wrote in his letter. A Mr Jude Alexander wants to buy into the Eastern — 'put you on a sound financial basis' were his exact words — and I refused.'

'No more money worries,' her father said. 'Sounds tempting.'

'And restrictive. Oh, Dad, you know

it would be awful, having a bean counter telling you how to run the company.'

'I expect you're right.' James George nodded absently, his mind already back in the dance studio where he had been working on his latest ballet. 'Are you off to the theatre now?'

'Yes, I've got to talk to the stage hands about their pay claim.' She pulled a face. 'I'm not looking forward to it because they do have a case. They don't earn much money — but none of us does, and we simply can't afford any more.'

* * *

An hour later she was saying as much to the stage hands' negotiator.

'I'm sorry, Stan, the money just isn't there.'

He was a morose man, and Gina rued the day, some sixteen months ago, that she had engaged him. It seemed to her that ever since then he had done

6

nothing but cause trouble, inciting the backstage crew to see grievances where before none had existed.

'That's all very well for you to say, Miss George, but my members are sick to death of excuses.'

They were standing side by side on the small stage of the Little Theatre, the home base of the Eastern Ballet Company. The footlights were on and cast pale pink pools around them; Gina would have asked the assistant stage manager to have turned them off, but it appeared Stan had cleared the theatre so the two of them could talk in private. This annoyed her because until his advent, problems had been brought directly to her and openly discussed with the whole crew until a solution was found, thus eliminating the situation she now felt they had of 'them' and 'us'.

'It's not an excuse, Stan, it's a fact.'

'In that case you will have to expect industrial action.'

She looked aghast. Their current

7

season included all the old favourites: *Swan Lake*, *Sleeping Beauty* and *Les Sylphides*, and had been expressly chosen to pull in the public. There was only one modern work, her father's *Shadows*, and even that was one of his earliest creations and considered a classic.

'If you go on strike, it follows that the company will go bankrupt, and then no one will have a job.' She didn't mince her words, yet oddly enough got the impression that the warning didn't worry him.

'I'll talk to my members,' he said and walked off stage.

'What a mess.' She was barely aware that she had spoken aloud. 'What am I going to do?'

'Accept my offer.' A dark brown voice came from the stalls.

She jumped, and shaded her eyes against the footlights as she tried to look beyond them to where the speaker stood.

The darkened form moved towards her, a tall figure with broad shoulders and a purposeful step. He climbed the stairs to the stage, and strode to her side.

'Jude Alexander,' he said without preamble, extending a large hand. 'I understand your bank manager spoke to you about me.'

His grip was firm and his smile friendly, but he struck her as someone used to getting his own way, who did not like being thwarted.

'Yes,' she agreed, 'he did mention your interest.'

'Interest?' He sounded irritated. 'I hope he put it a bit more strongly than that! I want to buy into your company.'

'Why?'

He seemed startled by her question and momentarily nonplussed, which astonished Gina, for she would have expected him to have looked at the investment from every angle and to have definite plans for how his money was to be used. And she really did want to know. Why would a successful businessman want to put money into what was, on paper at least, a failing ballet company?

He threw her an impatient look, heavy-lidded eyes flicking quickly over her, taking in the classical bun, slim figure and shapely dancer's legs. She felt uncomfortable under his inspection and frowned; this was a man used to asking the questions, she was sure, one not used to being grilled himself.

'I like a challenge,' he said at last. 'I've tried other businesses, now I'd like to give the arts a go.' He took a step closer and Gina, finding the sheer size of him intimidating, flinched slightly. He raised an eyebrow. 'You'll need to be stronger than that to stand up to the likes of Stan there. It seems I may have arrived in the nick of time.'

Gina felt her hackles rising. What an arrogant man! He seemed to think she should go down on her knees and thank heaven, fasting, for his intervention! Did he assume they would just accept his offer like that?

How rude of him to listen in on a

private conversation. But you only had to look at him to see that was the kind of person he was — hard-headed, forceful and demanding. She glared at his tough, strongly moulded face, and had a great desire to wipe the superior smile right off it.

'Goodness, our Fairy Godmother.' She smiled, too sweetly. 'Actually, it's very kind of you, Mr Alexander, but we've decided we'll muddle through without you.'

There was no mistaking that he was put out.

'You must be mad!' He didn't attempt to spare her feelings. 'I've asked around about the Eastern, made it my business to find out how things stand, and artistically you may be well thought of, but commercially — ' He gave an emphatic thumbs-down.

Gina found it hard to contain herself. So he thought them all washed up, did he? She could just imagine the type of theatre he would present if he got half a chance.

'Ballet is rarely a money-spinner,' she

11

said. 'I suggest you consider investing your money in musical comedy for a larger return.'

If she had meant to insult him, she didn't succeed, for he merely gave a great guffaw, of laughter. It was a pleasant sound from deep in his throat and quite startled Gina, who had expected him to be angry. He flung his head back as he laughed, giving her the chance to study his face.

His cheekbones were prominent and sharply angular, with a nose that was both too big and attractive, and a square, set jaw which gave him a fierce expression. A hard face, forceful even — softened as he laughed by a warm smile.

'See me as the Philistine grocer, do you?' he said when he had stopped laughing. As that was exactly what she had been thinking, she had the grace to blush, and hoped the pink footlights hid the fact. 'Well, maybe I am, at that, but I'm willing to learn, and whereas I realise this isn't the West End, I think I can improve your returns.'

'How? By feeding the audience a diet of *Coppelia* and *The Nutcracker* ad nauseam?'

Gina dripped sarcasm as she mentioned the two well-loved pot-boilers. Actually, she had nothing against either ballet, although she would have hated to have had them as a staple diet. She knew the company needed modern works as well if it was to grow, but presenting new ballets was a risk. Audiences were notoriously conservative in their taste, and preferred the traditional to the avant-garde.

'Isn't that what you're doing at the moment? As I understand it, your present programme could hardly be called adventurous.'

So he did know something about the ballet. Gina almost wished he didn't, for what he said was quite true, and she felt ashamed.

But popularity was not the only reason that the Eastern was presenting previous productions — money was tight, and there was none to spare for new costumes and sets. This way old props could be recycled.

'Our policy need not concern you, Mr Alexander,' she said with a haughty expression on her face. 'The Eastern is not for sale, and never will be.'

'Never is a long time, Miss George.' She could tell from his tone that he was irked by her attitude. 'I can afford to wait, but can you? While you prevaricate, the company is losing more and more money.'

She sensed he was a man who expected to get his own way, and was riled by his quiet assumption that he would win. She hoped he wouldn't come to look on the acquisition of the company as a challenge; she was not so naïve that she did not realise how difficult someone with all Jude Alexander's contacts could make things for them if he so chose.

'There is more to life than money,' she replied scathingly. She was over-reacting and knew it, but his cool self-possession got under her skin. How dared he assume everyone had their price?

It was true that the Eastern was in the red, but she disliked the way he was trying to bully her into accepting his terms. 'I won't be bamboozled into selling out on our ideals!'

'Don't be ridiculous!' He gave an impatient shake of his head and his heavy brows knitted. 'I thought psychotic ballerinas were only in films! I'm offering to help you, not rob you. Your father would retain artistic control of the company, I would simply be the administrator. I would have thought you'd be delighted to be released from all that paperwork.'

For one moment she was tempted. Oh, how she hated paperwork!

Then she noticed the mocking smile on Jude Alexander's lips. So he found her passion for the ballet amusing, did he? She glowered at him.

'We won't sell you the Eastern — not ever. Do you understand?'

The deep, melodious voice which

had first caught her attention when it boomed around the stalls, did not sound so attractive now.

'You're being a fool! Why on earth your father leaves a girl like you to run the business, I can't imagine. No wonder it's going downhill.' He shook his head in an exasperated fashion. 'You're too much of an innocent, Miss George.'

He could not have hurt her more had he hit her, and she turned away so that he could not see the pain well up in her eyes.

'Go away, Mr Alexander.' Her shoulders slumped. 'Just get out!'

She closed her eyes so didn't see his frown as he recognised the catch in her voice, nor the way he put out his hand as if to comfort her, before withdrawing his arm without making contact.

'As you wish. Goodbye for now, Miss George.'

She heard his footsteps retreating. *Goodbye for now* — he meant to return. He had not given the impression of someone who would take no for an answer.

16

She shivered; she had felt as threatened by the man himself as by his words. After all, such words were not new to her; someone else had called her *innocent* with that same air of contempt. Tears pricked her eyes. Perhaps it was true — perhaps she was stunted emotionally. Certainly she had hated what had happened between herself and David.

Hurriedly she dismissed the thought from her mind. *I won't remember, I won't*, she thought blindly, but even as she did so, the scene rose again in her mind's eye, and she knew she would never be free of it.

Bother Jude Alexander for encroaching on her carefully ordered life and reminding her of what she lacked! She wouldn't give him a second chance to get under her skin. She determined to instruct Paul Lindt to tell Mr Alexander in no uncertain terms that he was not welcome at the Little Theatre.

★ ★ ★

The rest of the day passed in the usual rush of rehearsals, office work and class. Madame Berthe, the ballet mistress of the company, was not pleased with Gina's progress and told her so after the lesson.

'Gina, you get worse, not better.' The elderly woman was stern. 'You skip too many classes.'

'Madame, I know, but I have to do so much more since mother died. There just aren't enough hours in the day.'

'Hmm — I blame James. He puts too much upon you.' It was a well-known fact that although the company belonged to James — or, more properly, to the bank since he had taken out that huge loan — it was his daughter who made most of the day-to-day decisions.

'It's not his fault.' Gina jumped to the defence of her father. 'Someone has to do it and he hasn't got the time.'

'Nor the inclination, it would appear. Your father has been spoiled — first your mother did all the hard work of actually running the company, and now he expects you to. It was all right for

Marjory, she liked doing the books and so on. You do not.'

At the mention of her mother's name, a great feeling of loss swept over Gina. The car crash that had taken her life had been two years ago, but still Gina missed her dreadfully.

'I do my best.'

'You would be better advised to give your best to the ballet. For a start, you are good at it — but you are not a good administrator.'

Gina knew it was true and dropped her head.

'But there's no one else — ' she protested

'Then employ someone.'

Even as she said it, Madame Berthe knew what the answer would be. James and his daughter were passionately devoted to the Eastern, and determined to preserve its independence at all costs. She quite understood that they should want to retain artistic control, of course; it was just a shame, in her opinion, that their undeniable talents did not extend to business acumen.

'Believe me, Gina, if you want to be a ballerina you will have to give up all other distractions. It is a strict life — ballet is a hard taskmaster — you cannot continue the way you are going.'

Gina felt helpless. She knew Madame Berthe was right, but how could she leave her father to run the company single-handedly?

She shook her head wryly as she imagined the chaos that would inevitably ensue if she did. James was a dreamer, a true artist, who while not despising the mundane matters of everyday life, hardly seemed to notice them.

This had not mattered when his wife had been alive; she was the business brain behind the enterprise. It had been thanks to her that the little group had flourished and the name James George had become renowned throughout the ballet world.

'I do want to dance — to work hard at my ballet. Once we've paid back the bank, I'll be able to take class more seriously.'

'By then it will be too late — and don't forget, when Alicia Allen retires at the end of the season the company will be without a first class ballerina. Oh, we have a number of promising soloists, but all our hopes were pinned on you.'

Gina felt guilt overwhelm her. It seemed she was letting everyone down. If only Alicia could be persuaded to stay on an extra year — but she knew that was impossible. The ballerina was in her early, forties now, and wanted to leave at her peak before her technique began to fail.

Indeed she had intended to go last year, but after the disastrous première of *Anna Karenina* and then David's defection, she had agreed to dance for one more season.

Gina noticed that Madame Berthe had used the past tense when talking about the company's hopes for her.

'I suppose after my performance as Anna, my future doesn't look quite so rosy,' she said, remembering the savaging the ballet had received at the hands of the critics. Unbidden, David's cruel words rose to taunt her.

'The failure of *Karenina* was not your fault,' Madame insisted. 'Surely you knew that? You were miscast and under-rehearsed, but considering you had to step in when Alicia strained a muscle, you gave a very creditable performance.'

'That's not what the critics thought.'

'The critics only made the point that you were very young — '

But that word stung Gina more than other, harsher ones might have done, and she interrupted before Madame Berthe could continue.

'Fonteyn danced her first *Giselle* at seventeen.'

'And at the same age you managed Odette in act two of *Swan Lake*, as I recall, when the guest artiste was rushed to hospital with appendicitis. That was when the press first dubbed you Swan Princess, wasn't it, because they said you were too young to be called Swan

22

Queen? They were most complimentary about your performance, as I remember, just pointing out that you would be even better with more experience.'

'Oh, yes, experience!'

Gina's bitter voice made the older woman look up with concern. She had known the girl all her life, and until last summer, had been sure nothing could cloud her sunny nature.

Even the tragic death of her mother had not broken her spirit; instead she had carried on, determined to continue Marjorie's work. Yet, since the *Karenina* debacle, Gina seemed a different person, lacking in confidence and distant, as if holding the world at bay.

'My dear Gina, artistes take risks every time they step on stage. Nothing is guaranteed in the theatre. You are going to have to learn to live with the critics.'

Oh, critics I can live with, Gina thought, *it was another's cruelty I can't forget.* But she didn't want to share her misery and forced a smile on her face.

Aloud she said, 'Madame, I have to go. The office — '

'I know, I know.' Madame Berthe held up her hand to stop the flow of words. 'But soon you will have to decide, one way or the other.'

She watched as the girl hurried away. She had been harsh, she knew, but she had to get through to her.

Gina made for the changing rooms, eager to escape the ballet mistress's shrewd scrutiny. She wanted to keep her shame and heartache private, and Madame Berthe knew her too well to be easily fooled.

Thus far most people seemed to think she had coped very well with David's desertion — that it had not hurt her deeply — and that was how she wanted it to stay. But then, they only knew half of the story, believing as they did that the reason David had left was to further his career, and that parting from his fiancée had been by mutual consent.

Only she knew the truth — knew her fatal flaw which had driven him away.

She clenched her fists, her nails

24

digging into her palms, using their sharp pain to block out a deeper, more destructive ache. Would it ever go, she wondered, or was, she doomed to carry the memory around with her for the rest of her life?

She caught sight of the clock on the wall, and realised she should be back in the office at the company's rehearsal rooms on the other side of the city. There was plenty to do — at least balancing the books took all her concentration and left her little time for brooding.

* * *

Yet on this occasion tackling the paperwork gave her a lot of cause for worry. As she added up the same column for the umpteenth time, and, reaching the same total, tried to decide which bills had to be paid immediately and which ones she could decently leave for another month, she knew the company could not stave off disaster for very much longer.

What were they going to do? She twisted her fingers through her long, straight ponytail, and stared out of the window at the river at the bottom of the garden and the wild jungle in between — her mother's favourite place to relax.

'I do love it here, don't you?' she always said as she and Gina sat sipping iced lemonade under a tree, and Gina had. Hidden from the view of neighbours by the wild, overgrown garden, her mother by her side, she had felt loved and protected and safe, as if nothing could ever hurt her. And it was to this wilderness of shrubs, wild flowers and tangled ivy, that she would come to think whenever anything portentous occurred, crisp lettuce leaves in her hands to attract the regal swans that glided by.

'We must have a shot of you in your Odette costume with the swans!' Marjory had an eye for publicity, and knew a photo opportunity when she saw one. And so it was that Gina had posed in her short white tutu and feathered headdress and crown with the magnificent birds, just as had Anna Pavlova years before.

The headline that accompanied the newspaper report was *Swan Princess captures all hearts*, and the name had stuck.

Georgina George, soloist with the Eastern Ballet, with friends. Miss George, who danced her first Swan Lake last night, is the daughter of choreographer James George and his wife Marjory, who set up the Eastern Ballet Company twenty years ago when Mrs George inherited the large Regency house in Boundary Road from her parents.

When asked where the idea to start a company came from, Mrs George said, 'James wanted to choreograph full length, three-act ballets, but it would have taken years for him to get the chance if he had stayed working for an established company. I believed in my husband, and as always, dear James believed in me, and so he resigned from the Royal Ballet. That was a big step because it is such a prestigious company, but it meant he was able to start creating the ballets he wanted to.'

The last of Marjory's mother's legacy was used to buy the old derelict Roxy Cinema. The company had to tour for some years before they were able to afford to renovate it and make it their base.

From looking at family albums, Gina knew that in her grandparents' day the back garden had been neat and well-tended. However as neither Marjory nor her husband had had the time or inclination for gardening, it had become a wildlife haven long before such things were fashionable.

The small terrace had survived — crumbling and slightly faded — but still a pleasant place to sit on a fine day, and tears stung Gina's eyes as she remembered her mother, papers on the table in front of her, doing the accounts there.

'We could probably afford to have it landscaped now,' Marjory said one day.

'What do you think?'

Gina had been horrified. 'That would be awful.'

Marjory roared with laughter, and Gina realised it was just another of her mother's teases. She bent down and laced her arms around her mother's neck.

'I'd hate it, too. I do my best thinking in this garden. It was here I had the vision to set up the ballet company for your dad and convert the majority of the house into a professional ballet school. People said we were mad, that cramming my family into a small flat in the basement would break up my marriage, and that East Anglia wasn't big enough to sustain a professional dance troupe, but we proved them wrong.'

'I'm so glad you did. It can't have been easy.'

People might talk of her father's talents in awed tones, but Gina knew how much was owed to his wife. Whereas James was all artistic endeavour, Marjory was vibrant, capable and businesslike, and it was these skills as much as James' more admired artistic abilities that had made the Eastern Ballet the success it was.

'No, but we got there in the end.'

There was pride in Marjory's voice — and no wonder, thought Gina. She had founded the company from scratch and kept it on a sound financial footing, all to ensure her husband had what she believed he most deserved — his own ballet company. That it had gone from strength to strength was due to both James' artistic direction and Marjory's shrewd financial brain.

'You did indeed!' Gina leaned over and gave her mother a kiss.

'I've got something to tell you. Things are going so well for us that I've given James the go-ahead to stage *Anna Karenina*.' Her mother was obviously bursting to share the news. 'You know how long he's wanted to make a ballet of the famous Russian novel? Well, finally, the time is right. Things couldn't look better for the company — we have an international reputation, a fine line-up of top flight performers, and our financial situation is sound.'

Gina remembered the excitement in the company when the new ballet began to take shape, for when James finally came to create it, he pulled out all the stops. This was to be the culmination of all their work together — but Marjory hadn't lived to see its completion, and although she would give anything to have her mother back, Gina was glad she had not lived to see how the expected triumph turned to disaster.

She gave a deep sigh and dragged her thoughts back to the present. If the stage-hands did go on strike, the company would be in real trouble — but would they? The Eastern had always been such a tightly knit company, with everyone, from the lowliest cleaner to the great Alicia Allen, mucking in and pulling their weight, that it was hard for her to understand the backstage crew's ultimatum.

Things were not going too well, it was true, but always before in a crisis they had been at pains to help out. What was it that had changed them?

It must be me, she thought — for try as she might to explain it away, the only difference today was that she was in charge.

She was not the type of person to lie to herself; Marjory had been one of those happy people whom everyone loved, and had been looked on by all the company as a kind of Earth Mother. Gina knew she was not held in the same esteem.

For a few months after her mother had died things had seemed to continue as normal, but then came *Karenina*, and whatever family feeling had remained was finally lost. They had had to find a replacement for David and a temporary stand-in until Alicia recovered; a couple of stagehands had retired and new ones were employed; but apart from that, the original company remained. Perhaps the shock of quite so stunning a failure had made people wonder about the safety of their jobs in so precarious a ballet company.

Gina closed her eyes to think. If only she could see her way out of their problems: if only her mother had not died, if only David had not left, if only Alicia were not retiring. So many if-onlys, and all of them futile. Life was hard and often cruel (she knew, she had been taught by a master of the art) and fairytale endings only happened in ballets like *Sleeping Beauty*.

'What am I going to do?' She repeated her earlier cry without thinking, and saw again the tall, broad-shouldered figure with his strong, assertive face and crooked smile.

'No!' She brought her fist down heavily on the desk in front of her. She remembered how he had watched her through those dark, heavy-lidded eyes, his lantern jaw set in an expression of cynical amusement. She grudgingly allowed that he could not help his aggressive masculinity, but recognised he was the type of man with whom she would always be ill at ease. She could not imagine being able to strike up a happy working relationship with him.

'Something better will come up.'

She said it more in desperation than belief, for she could not bear to think of another man wheedling his way into the Eastern as David had done. Especially one she found as pushy and arrogant as Jude Alexander.

2

A few days later, Gina only just arrived at the theatre in time for the half-hour call. She had meant to get there early enough for a warm up before the performance, but had buried herself so deeply in the problems of the company, that she had almost missed her bus.

'Good evening, Ted.' She smiled at the elderly stage doorman as she entered, but although he gave her a curt nod, he did not return her greeting.

Odd, she thought. Ted was usually the most garrulous of souls — perhaps he had had a bad day. But she had no time to dwell on his problems, real or imaginary, for she had to get ready.

She hurried to the tiny boxroom which served as but did not deserve the title of dressing-room, and felt a rush of possessive pride as she entered. Felicity Hawes, a fellow soloist, shared it with her, and was already dressed and waiting to go on stage.

'You're cutting it a bit fine.'

'I know, I forgot the time.'

The familiarity of her methodical preparations steadied Gina's nerves. She quickly pulled on her tights and tied the ribbons on her pink satin pointe shoes, neatly tucking away the unsightly ends. She pulled her hair back into an unembellished classical bun, and then slapped her arms and chest with wet-white body Pancake make-up.

'Would like me to do your back?'

'Please.' Gina handed Felicity the sponge she had been using as an applicator. They were presenting three one-act ballets that evening, and Gina was dancing in two of them: the Mazurka in *Les Sylphides* and the Second Girl in *Shadows*. It was for the former that she needed to look pale and ethereal, hence the wet-white. Sylphs were meant to be other-worldy, not bronzed modern women, and as she worked the Pancake into her arms, she took on the ghostly pallor which would look so spiritual under the blue lights.

'There you are — done! I'll go on stage now and leave you to it — be easier if you have more room. Honestly, this theatre is the most cramped, uncomfortable — '

'No it isn't!'

But even as she defended it, Gina knew what Felicity had said was nothing but the truth. The Little Theatre was probably one of the ugliest theatres in the world, yet she could not have loved another half as well. It had started life as a cinema in the thirties, but soon had proved too small to make a reasonable profit, and became a dance hall during the Second World War. Then, after being left derelict for some years, it became in turn a bingo house, a seedy nightclub, and finally, when Marjorie George had discovered and bought it, a furniture repository.

A less likely ballet venue it would have been hard to find, and its situation, in an area designated for slum clearance, was appalling. But Marjory, with that mixture of foresight and luck that seemed to touch everything she did, insisted on buying it, and was proved right when the conversion resulted in a comfortable auditorium with excellent seating, and a stage exactly right for a company the size of the Eastern. That backstage was cramped and not very salubrious had not mattered to her; it was the audience who needed to be relaxed and at ease, not the dancers.

Gina slipped on a light housecoat, and began applying the thick stage make-up she loathed wearing but knew she must.

'Hello, Princess.' Her father popped his head around the door. He had been proud when she had earned the title Swan Princess and had shortened it affectionately. 'Came to wish you good luck.' He looked tired and drawn, and Gina wondered what his real reason for dropping in was. Usually he was far too involved prior to a performance to make social calls.

'Are you OK, Dad? Come and sit

down for a moment until I put on my costume.'

That James agreed to do so worried her, too. It was so unlike him not to be fussing around the stage with last-minute details.

'I'm all right, darling, it's you I'm concerned about.' He sat forward in the chair to study her face. 'You're doing too much and your dancing is suffering.'

Madame Berthe must have caught him and spoken to him, Gina thought, and she hurried to reassure him. 'Oh, I'm fine, really. The paperwork is a bit time-consuming, but don't you worry, we'll be out of the woods by the end of the season.'

'Will we?' A mixture of doubt and relief flooded his face, and the relief salved her conscience about telling him a lie.

Well, not a lie exactly — she still prayed that somehow she would be able to get them out of this mess, but why trouble her father with the details? He

39

would find out soon enough if they did go to the wall, and if they didn't, well, he would have been saved unnecessary worry.

It was her failure that had brought them to the edge of the abyss after all, and now she felt it her duty to protect this gentle man, just as her mother had done before her.

'Of course.' She smiled indulgently as if she, rather than he, were the parent.

'I'm glad. But if that's the case, you really must spend more time on your ballet. Don't forget the old saying: 'Miss class one day and you notice the difference, miss class two days and the company notices, miss class three days and the audience becomes aware'.'

She nodded. It was true, and she had overheard comments about her somewhat ropey performance from other dancers and also the fans who milled around the stage door as she left the theatre each evening. Her father must have observed her falling standard, too, though she didn't believe he would be aware that she was skipping classes unless someone had told him the fact, and she hoped Madame hadn't done so.

Actually, she acknowledged, her deterioration must have started long before she began to miss lessons — hadn't *Karenina* proved that? Her father's crowning creation on which he had staked his all, and which had been expected to be hailed as a masterpiece.

And it so nearly came off, she thought, *and that it didn't was all my fault!* She curled forward as if protecting herself as she remembered the ghastly opening night which should have made the company's fortune, and instead plunged it into debt, and the all too familiar feeling of guilt rose to assail her.

The worst of it was her belief that she had let her parents down — had ruined her father's dream and damaged her mother's reputation, for everyone knew *Karenina* was the last production Marjory had been involved with.

'Are you all right, Gina?' Her father had noticed her expression and was eyeing her with concern.

'Yes, I'm fine, thanks. Just a twinge of stage fright.' She couldn't let him know what was really troubling her, because he would simply deny she'd had anything to do with the failure.

Somehow, the fact that no one apart from David had blamed her had made it even more unbearable. They had all been anxious not to add to her distress, coming so soon after her mother's death. David had suffered from no such reservations — which was understandable considering how close they were and how near she had come to wrecking his career — and had told her in no uncertain terms just what she had done. She had been horrified when she'd realised the truth, and had tried to apologise to her father.

'Don't fret, Swan Princess. I should never have allowed you to dance Anna,' was all he had ever said — which had merely served to prove to her, if proof had been needed, that it was indeed down to her that the ballet had been a flop.

Was that why she didn't feel as close to her father these days as she used to? Because she knew he would only make excuses for her, and she couldn't bear to feel she was being humoured? She might be young, but she was old enough to take responsibility for her own actions, and didn't expect others to take the blame.

However she had felt the need to make up to her father for what her failure had cost him, and so had gradually released him from the burden of office work to let him concentrate on the ballet, even though it meant she was not able to do the same. She realised that had subtly changed their relationship: she came to see his lack of worldly wisdom in a different, less attractive light.

She found it hard to admit even to herself — brought up as she had been by a man who always seemed to be on a higher plane — but sometimes the thought of having someone strong and proactive, someone who took decisive action, was very appealing.

'Oh, by the way,' James said as he rose to leave, 'you'll be having visitors backstage during the interval.' He saw the frown she gave and hurried on. 'The bank manager is here with a party. With the size of our overdraft, we daren't upset him!'

So that was why James looked so tense, Gina realised as he left the room — the bank manager must have been having a chat with him. She hoped not too much had been said, but then her father was pretty financially illiterate, so he probably hadn't taken in a lot. Whereas if it had been her mother, she would have been shocked to see the shaky position in which the Eastern now found itself.

'Overture and beginners, ladies and gentlemen. Beginners on stage, please.'

The stage manager's voice boomed over the tannoy, and she pushed all such worrying thoughts from her mind as she prepared to enter the dreamy world of *Les Sylphides*.

She danced her best, but knew in her heart it was not good enough, and that hurt. Once she had been very confident about her performances, knowing the agonising daily classes helped towards a faultless technique, and believing her emotional range to be wide.

Now she knew she was wrong on both counts. The fire and attack with which she used to dance were today beyond her, and as for the depths of emotion — David had long since disabused her of any belief she might have had on that score.

You're cold, do you hear me? Glacial, like a block of ice! The hateful words echoed around her brain, and she had to acknowledge that he knew best. He was, after all, older and more experienced than she . . . and however much she had tried to block out what he had said, the newspapers the next morning had merely repeated the accusation.

45

Last night Georgina George danced the part of Anna Karenina as a child rather than a woman.

Every critic had said much the same, and all had agreed she was too young and inexperienced for the role.

Gina wandered disconsolately to her dressing-room. She guessed, correctly, that most of the visitors would want to meet the more famous Alicia Allen, and so slipped out of the *Sylphides'* flowing romantic tutu, and pulled on her old dressing-gown. She brushed her hair loosely down her back ready for her next performance, and was just retouching her make-up when there was a knock at the door.

'Come in.'

He was wearing a formal dinner suit, and had it been on anyone but him, she would have been delighted. She liked it when people dressed up for the theatre, it showed they had made an effort, just as those on stage were doing. But him!

She scowled at Jude Alexander's towering frame — he seemed even taller than she remembered — and found herself tensing as he squeezed into the small dressing-room.

'What are you doing here?' she demanded, confused by his arrival. 'You'll have to go — I'm expecting visitors.'

Once across the threshold he paused for a moment, focusing on her slight frame, as if mesmerised. She felt vulnerable and exposed, and pulled her flimsy robe more tightly around herself.

'I know, I'm one of them — your visitors, I mean. May I?' Without waiting for an answer he went to sit on the small shabby chaise longue in the corner of the room. Cleo, the theatre cat, was sleeping in her usual place, and Gina waited with glee for the inevitable explosion.

'Hello, puss.' He bent to pick her up gently. 'Is there room for another?'

Cleo stretched, all languid movement, and royally allowed her chin to be tickled. Then she settled down, satisfied, on Jude Alexander's lap.

Gina stared in disbelief; usually any

47

disturbance turned the cat into a spitting virago. Her eyes met those of the tamer, and she realised he had worked out what she had expected to happen and was laughing at her.

She took a deep breath to count to ten, and instead was assailed by a clean, sharp smell — a mixture of pine and cologne which she recognised as the après rasage he had worn that afternoon. And there was something else, something more basic and exciting, and — well — male.

She blinked, taken aback by her discovery.

'The ballet was beautiful.' Jude Alexander leaned towards her, and she felt a small pulse of fear begin in her head, beating just as surely as he was trying to beat down her objections to his proposal. She resisted an urge to flee from the room, and tried to laugh off the defensive expression she knew he had seen.

'That's all you know! I danced abominably.'

She was aware she was overreacting, yet seemed unable to stop herself. He brought out the worst in her, and she believed attack was the best form of defence. She was conscious that her face was too open and revealed too much — yet another fault of the innocent and naïve, she thought — and she wanted to give nothing away. Not to this man, who might use it against her.

'You could do with more practice,' he agreed, showing her once again he was not the complete ballet novice she had initially taken him for. 'I suspect you try to do too much — you can't both run a company and be its leading lady.'

'Oh, and as a grocer you know all about ballet companies?' She didn't try to hide her scorn, but the attack did not seem to bother him.

'As a managing director I know about running a company successfully, and this I tell you for nothing: it's impossible to do two time-consuming jobs well. You know it yourself, if you're truthful — the Eastern is not in a good position business-wise, and you are dancing no more than adequately.'

She looked daggers at him, furious that what he said was so patently true.

A voice from the open doorway saved her from having to make a reply.

'There you are, Jude!' Mrs Lindt, the bank manager's wife was as tall and thin as her husband was short and portly, and they made an odd pair in their evening finery.

'You two know each other?'

'Of course, m'dear,' Mr Lindt said, and gave her a pompous look. 'When Mr Alexander approached me about investing in the Eastern, I mentioned it to Helen,' he nodded towards his wife, 'and she invited him for Sunday lunch. She, like him, is very keen on the ballet, you see. Indeed, if I'd have let her, I'm sure she'd have wanted to attend the meeting I had this afternoon with him and your father to discuss the Eastern.'

Gina was furious. She saw her father standing outside in the corridor and threw him a questioning glance. He shrugged sheepishly and hung his shoulders in defeat.

So that was why he had looked so downcast earlier in her dressing-room! Jude Alexander had been haranguing him. Having realised she was resolute in her determination not to allow him to become a part the Eastern, he must have underhandedly approached her father and used the inside knowledge he had gathered — that she was not making a good job of the administration and her performances were suffering because of skipping classes — to coax James onto his side.

She cursed herself as a fool. She should have suspected something when James first came to her. It was so unlike him to check up on whether she had attended class, she should have realised someone had put him up to it, and that someone wasn't Madame Berthe!

No wonder he had looked so guilty — she could just imagine Jude Alexander subtly blaming James for working his daughter too hard. But she would not let him win, she would not!

'We've persuaded your father to have dinner with us tomorrow, so we can discuss it further.' Mr Lindt beamed, his bald pate gleaming under the bare electric light bulb. 'I understand you won't be performing then, so we would be glad if you could accompany him. The bank's annual dinner-dance . . . a car will call for you.'

He ushered his party out, happy to have convinced himself all was well. Her father followed, leaving her alone again with Jude Alexander.

'How dare you!' She turned on him immediately. 'How dare you harass my father? I told you we were not interested in your offer, and you had no right to approach him behind my back!'

'No right?' He shot her an enquiring look, his brow furrowed and dark eyes narrowing. 'While we're talking about rights, do you ever consider those of your father? It is his company, not yours, yet you insist on treating him like a little boy.'

'I do not!' But the barb had hit home; sometimes it did feel as if she had to mother James. The knowledge made her lash out with a pointed response. 'It's just that he's not as suspicious as I am and sees good in everyone, however undeserving!'

He studied her face dispassionately.

'You've already made your opinion of me more than clear,' he said, 'and I can live with it. Have you ever considered how your father lives with your opinion of him?'

'I love him — he knows that!'

'You may love him, but you also smother him. You try to remove every obstacle from his path as if he is quite incapable of coping with even the most mundane of tasks.'

'You don't understand. My mother did everything for James, he'd be totally lost — '

She broke off, angry with herself for trying to justify her actions to this self-important man. Her family arrangements were nothing to do with him, and she opened her mouth to say so, but he did not give her the chance.

'That was different — they were married and had decided how their relationship worked best. You are his daughter, and you are doing your best to emasculate him.'

An angry flush came to her face, his cool words penetrating her self-control.

'That's a horrible thing to say!'

But she was remembering all too vividly that other occasion when someone else had accused her of doing something similar to him.

'It's not a very nice thing to do,' he said levelly, only the tone of his voice showing he thought her reactions overdone and unnecessary. 'Don't try to recreate what your father had with your mother. You can't — don't you see? It's impossible to judge or analyse a successful relationship, it just happens. If you continue to try and replace all your mother did, you'll detract from what they had together, and no one should come between a man and his woman.'

She understood then. *His woman*, he had said, as if a wife wasn't a person in her own right, but merely an appendage! It was clear Jude Alexander was a man who expected women to pay full homage to his masculinity, and not take, as had her mother, the position of command.

'It's you who is blind,' she said crisply. 'You can't see that marriage is an equal partnership, not a captain and mate situation.'

He shrugged. 'I know you can't have two commanders and still win the battle. But we were talking about your father — '

'You were talking about my father, trying to blame me for the fact that he always is preoccupied with his choreography. But what really bugs you is that he lets a woman run the company, isn't it?'

'I don't care who runs a company, so long as they do so well. You do not.'

She knew it was the truth but still seethed inwardly. How very like a man, to bring things down to abuse! But a little voice inside her would not let such unfairness pass; Jude Alexander was merely stating a fact, and it was she who had brought the conversation down to a personal level and given him the opening in the first place.

She sighed — sometimes she wished she could be like Princess Aurora in *Sleeping Beauty* and fall asleep for a hundred years. Surely by then all their problems would be solved?

As if he sensed her depression, he moved towards her, grasping her upper arms firmly in his large hands.

'What are you trying to prove?' he demanded. 'That you are a superwoman? There's no dishonour in accepting that one is not an expert at everything. Do what you are good at — dance! You can't wipe away the past by doing penance with your future.'

His perception stunned her. It was true, she had tried to blot out all that had happened since *Karenina*, and was attempting to make up for its failure by being a jack of all trades — and as a result, she was master of none. His words made sense, yet she was loath to admit it.

It's as if he is hypnotising me, she thought, thoroughly distracted and aware of an electric tingling where his fingers were biting into her flesh. She felt as if she were completely paralysed, unable to push him away or to turn and make her escape herself. Her legs were like jelly, and she balled her hands into small fists by her sides as she tried to fight the feeling of being swamped.

He stared deep into her eyes. *He's trying to read my mind*, she panicked, *trying to find information to use against me. But I won't weaken — won't be overwhelmed by his predatory male act!*

'This is your five-minute call, ladies and gentlemen, your five-minute call.'

At the sound of the disembodied voice she jumped away, and he made no move to keep her.

'I'll leave you to get ready,' he said smoothly. 'See you tomorrow night.'

She stared after his departing figure.

Why should he have affected her like that, she wondered, when she had never trembled at David's touch? Remembering David made her realise the answer to her question — his description of her lack of prowess as a fiancée, and a woman, had made her wary of all men. The tingling when Jude Alexander had held her must have been a warning from her subconscious to back off.

These days she was uncomfortable about her own feelings, afraid to allow anyone to get too close in case they saw the inner failings her outward appearance managed to hide.

* * *

The applause at the end of her solo in *Shadows* was loud and appreciative, and for once she felt she had earned it. Her father had created the role of the Second Girl expressly for her when she was still in her early teens, and had not risked distressing her with steps that were too advanced for her capabilities, but had left her free to take on the emotion of the young lover. Her spontaneity and gaiety shone through the easy choreography; years of interpretation in the part had made it uniquely her own.

'Well done, Gina!' Madame Berthe was delighted. 'Just when I am ready to despair of you, your talent breaks through to excite me all over again!'

Gina smiled, and buried her head in the glorious bouquet of red roses she had received on stage as she took her curtain call. She noticed a card attached to the stems, and peered at it in the dimmed light of the wings.

I look forward to working with you, it said in a firm, spiky hand, and was signed *Jude Alexander*.

All the happiness she had been feeling immediately dissolved, as she remembered his determined efforts to take over the Eastern. Now, more than ever, she knew she could never work comfortably with him, and his single-minded pursuit of his aims frightened her. What overweening conceit to write to her as if the deal were already signed and sealed.

She squared herself up and marched to her dressing-room — the fight had just begun!

3

The next morning, it seemed to her that the gods were not on her side.

'Swan Princess, darling,' her father croaked, 'I feel quite dreadful. It must be this awful flu that's about. I won't be able to go to the dinner-dance tonight.'

'Never mind.' She beamed. 'I didn't want to go anyway.'

James started a coughing fit, and when he had finished, he grabbed her wrists.

'Princess, you must go! We daren't risk alienating Mr Lindt!'

Gina grimaced, but seeing her father watching her so anxiously, she put on a brilliant smile.

'Don't worry, Dad, I'll go if you want me to.'

She was rewarded by a grateful look, but inside she was furious. Bother Jude Alexander, why did he have to come along and upset their equilibrium? She decided she would leave the dance as early as was politely possible — she had no intention of listening to his proposals for a moment longer than was necessary.

Luckily, he would undoubtedly be with a girlfriend, whom she hoped might cramp his style, while she was a free agent and could come and go as she pleased.

The next problem she had to overcome was what to wear. She went into her tiny, neat bedroom and opened the wardrobe. She was not a fashionista, and most of the time wore the universal dancer's uniform of leotard and tights with just an old pair of jeans and a jumper thrown over them when she went to the theatre. She gave a wry smile — not quite the thing to wear out with Jude Alexander.

She drew herself up — what did it matter if she didn't come up to his expensive taste? She was not trying to impress him, rather the reverse. Since David, she had done her best to avoid attracting the attention of the opposite sex, knowing as she did that whatever they might believe she promised, in reality she would turn out to be a bitter disappointment.

She pushed the row of trousers to one side, and pulled out her smarter outfits from the deeper recesses of the cupboard. There were a couple of cotton sundresses, an elegant suit she had bought to wear when attending business meetings, and the pair of skin-tight black trousers and lace top she had worn to the party after the first night of *Anna Karenina*. David had said it was a tease, because it made her look like a real woman, when in fact she was like the fairy in *Le Baiser De La Fée* — the heartless ice maiden from the Hans Christian Andersen story.

She slammed the wardrobe door, eager to hide the evidence that the awful night had ever occurred. *I should have thrown them away*, she thought. But she had kept them for a purpose — a reminder, if such she needed, not to allow herself to get close to a man ever again.

'Gina, are you there?' Madame Berthe called from the front door of the flat.

'Here, Madame.' Gina went to meet her. 'I was just trying to decide what to wear tonight. Dad has told you about the dinner-dance, I suppose?'

'Yes, and I am so glad. You need the chance to relax.'

'It's hardly relaxation where Jude Alexander is concerned — more a business meeting.'

'Really?' The older woman looked sceptical. 'He seemed a very sociable man to me.'

Gina was still distracted about what she was going to wear, and not paying a great deal of attention. 'Hmm? I didn't realise you knew him. Anyway, whether he is or not is immaterial unless I can find a suitable outfit for the occasion.'

'That's easily solved. What about the black velvet costume from *Anna Karenina*?'

Gina was taken aback by the suggestion. She never would have dreamed of using a ballet costume — most of them were far too theatrical to be worn offstage — but Madame Berthe certainly had a point. The dress she suggested was one Anna had worn when visited by her husband to discuss the future of their son, and as the scene had been mainly mime, was not subject to the usual constraints of ballet costumes: skirts no longer than ankle length, loose for ease of movement and light to dance in. But even as she considered it, she dismissed the idea — the ballet had too many unhappy associations.

'No, it won't do — ' she began, but Madame Berthe hushed her with a look.

'Rubbish, it will look beautiful, especially if you team it with the cloak you wore for the suicide scene. I'll get them out of wardrobe and take them to the two-hour cleaners in St Agnes Street.' She gave a sharp nod of her head which brooked no interference, and was gone.

Gina stood in the doorway and nibbled her thumb. It was true, the dress had been wonderful and she knew it had suited her. With the cloak it would not look out of place tonight — but could she stand wearing a reminder of her greatest failure, both as a woman and as a dancer?

Perhaps it was time to lay the ghost, she allowed — and anyway, she had nothing else to wear. She didn't want to give Jude Alexander the satisfaction of knowing she couldn't afford a new evening dress; he would see it as further example of her poor husbandry, and if she cried off with any other excuse, he would think she was afraid of him and would believe he had won.

* * *

That evening, as she inspected her reflection in front of the mirror, she was glad she had not given in. She had swept her hair up into a pile of curls high on her head, which showed off her

66

fine features and swan-like neck, and the dress, in rich black velvet, looked perfect. She swung the crimson-lined cape around her, and wondered if the muff that accompanied it would be too much . . . but, no, it was so obviously meant that she slipped a handkerchief inside it and forewent a handbag.

'You look beautiful, my dear.' The ballet mistress clasped her hands in delight. 'Ah, there's the doorbell. Now go and enjoy yourself.'

Gina had expected the bank to send a car to pick her up, and was quite startled to open the door and find Jude Alexander on the step. He was dressed in a dark dinner jacket again, the formality of which sat easily upon him, and she was startled to find herself admitting he was quite attractive in an unconventional sort of way. His features were too strong, his expression too assertive to earn him the title 'handsome', but his hard-boned face and muscular frame added up to a very imposing man.

He started when he saw her, giving her a look of such burning intensity, straight up and down, that she wondered if her outfit was overdone.

'You look magnificent,' was all he said, and his tone indicated approval. 'I feel very fortunate to have such an attractive partner.'

'Partner?' She eyed him suspiciously. 'What do you mean? If you've been bothering my father again when he is so unwell, and persuaded him to accept your offer — '

He held up his hand to silence her.

'Relax! I meant partner as in dancing companion, not business associate, and I don't recall ever having 'bothered' your father.'

She felt rather stupid for having leapt to the wrong conclusion, but was thrown by the fact he was to be her escort to the dinner-dance.

'I wasn't expecting you to accompany me,' she said. 'You didn't have to, you know, I could quite easily have gone on my own.'

'I know I didn't have to, but I wanted to.' He took her by the arm and escorted her to the waiting red Porsche.

She pursed her lips at his words, disbelief quite evident, for she knew men found her childish and undesirable. Magical Swan Princess she might be, but a real-life warm and wanted woman — that was beyond her. She was sure he was aware of that detail and was merely trying to soften her up, trying to break down the barriers and get her to agree to his proposition.

'I'm quite capable of opening a door on my own,' she said ungraciously as he ushered her into the car. 'Dancers may look ethereal, but in reality, we are stronger than most athletes.'

He gave a mocking bow of his head.

'And I may look like an ignorant oaf, but I happen to believe in good manners. Let me help you with your seat belt.' He leaned across her to do so, but she didn't complain, for she saw he was only doing it to annoy her.

And is managing to do so, she

thought with a tight smile, although she strove not to show him. His face came closer to hers as he studied the clasp, and she shrank back in her seat, pushing her spine as far back against it as she could.

Why was she afraid? Because he might be able to overcome her resistance? Surely not.

She dismissed the thought, but found it more difficult to dismiss her quivering anxiety. She watched him from under her thick, curling lashes, taking in the slight blue shadow on his chin, the determined set of his mouth and the small creases around his eyes, which showed that contrary to her experience, he was no stranger to laughter.

'Are you OK?' He must have felt her disquiet.

'Of course!' she snapped. 'Why shouldn't I be?'

'No reason.' He closed the car door.

He drove well, fast but within the limit and without cutting corners. She wondered if he did his business in the same manner — then realised she already knew the answer to that. The only reason he was with her tonight was to try and persuade her to change her mind and let him buy into the Eastern. However pleasant he might appear to be, he was only being so for his own cynical ends, and she was not taken in by it. She knew a man like him would not be attracted to her, whatever impression he gave.

He pulled up at red traffic lights, and leaned over to pluck a piece of fluff from her cloak. She shrank back.

'Relax, Gina! Ever since we met you've been like a cat on hot bricks. Do you suspect all men of devious behaviour, or am I alone singled out for the dubious honour of being after your bones?'

'It may surprise you to know not every girl wants to fall in a panting heap at your feet!' she said as the lights changed. She stared at his profile as he drove. 'If that's what you expected from me, you're out of luck! Ballet is my life, and it is one of severe discipline and plain, unromantic hard work. I have no time for anything else.'

'Yet in spite of ballet being your passion, your dancing is slipping — you yourself told me so.'

That he was right infuriated her, but before she could respond he continued. 'Perhaps you spend too much time on business and not enough on ballet.' He took his eyes off the road for a moment to look at her and she bit her lip and hurriedly turned away.

'Look,' she said when he was safely facing the front again, 'can we agree not to discuss the Eastern tonight? Neither of us wants to be here — you simply see it as a way to butter me up to get your own way, and I'm only humouring my father. Let's accept we've got to spend the next three hours or so together and call a truce. We may not like each other, but at least we can be civilised about it.'

Actually, she doubted he could. He wore his leader-of-the-pack masculinity like a badge, and she suspected if put to the test, it would be the veneer of a gentleman that would go first, not his potent machismo.

'So, you can read minds, too,' he said caustically. 'By all means let's keep to the pleasantries of life, though I never thought of you as a coward.'

She would have asked him what he meant, but at that moment the car swept through a pair of ornate wrought iron gates and drew up outside the hotel. A doorman helped her from the car, and she climbed nervously up the broad stone steps to the doorway while Jude parked.

She was not used to such places. It was true what she had told him — until David, her life had consisted of a relentless dedication to work and her social life had revolved around the company. It had been fun, but it rarely included dates at expensive hotels.

'Georgina, my dear.' Mrs Lindt had seen her hovering uncertainly by the door and bore down upon her. 'Where's Jude?'

'Parking the car.'

'Well, come with me and I'll show you where to leave that beautiful cloak.' She took the girl and led her by the arm to the cloakroom. Then, 'Oh, look, there's my husband. John — take Gina to our table, will you, while I wait here for Jude?'

Mr Lindt processed into the ballroom. Gina noticed people staring at her and hoped her dress was not too obviously a costume, unconscious of the aura of elegance that surrounded her.

'Hope they don't play too loudly,' Mr Lindt joked as he sat her at a table next to the band, and she nodded her agreement. 'Actually, I'm pleased to have this opportunity to talk to you alone,' the bank manger continued. 'Jude seems to be under the impression you still aren't keen for him to join you at the Eastern.'

'I'm not.'

He blinked behind his pebble-glass spectacles.

'But now you've had time to think about it, why ever not?' he demanded. 'It's like a gift from the gods, surely you can see that?'

'I don't think so.'

'Miss George,' he said, all formality now, his earlier intimacy forgotten, 'I really don't think you should be flippant. Your company owes the bank a very great deal of money, with no way of paying it back in the foreseeable future. Please don't allow what appears to be a personality clash to cloud your judgment — ' He stopped as Jude and Mrs Lindt approached.

'I was just telling Gina how fortuitous is your offer,' he told Jude in a firm voice once everyone was seated.

'I doubt she agreed with you.' Jude gave a weary smile. 'Still, don't let's talk shop tonight.'

Mrs Lindt nodded her agreement while her husband looked crestfallen. Clearly his idea of enjoyment was to discuss business.

'Thank you,' Gina murmured as Jude

passed her a glass of champagne.

'What for?'

'Keeping your word and not talking business.'

He grinned. 'Oh, I know how to behave in polite society with the best of them,' he said. 'In fact, you might find I'm halfway decent if you ever let me get close enough to prove it.'

She gave him a startled look, unsure of which way to take him.

'Come on. Let's dance.' He rose to his feet.

'I can't.' Gina was embarrassed to admit it. 'Not proper, *Strictly*-type dancing.'

'A ballet dancer who can't waltz? I don't believe it!' His face relaxed into an incredulous smile.

'It's true, it's very different from ballet, and I've never learned how.'

'Then I shall teach you. Just follow my lead.'

Not likely, she thought, but allowed herself to be taken on to the dance floor, and jumped nervously as he put

76

his arms around her.

'I won't attack you, Gina — at least,' he flashed a theatrical leer, 'not here in front of everyone. Just relax.'

She tried to do so, but found it difficult. She was very aware of his closeness, and her body trembled as she conceded her weakness.

He proved an excellent teacher, guiding her around the floor with expert timing, and she whirled and turned to his lead as she never would have done had they not been dancing.

'You're good,' he flattered her, 'though that is hardly surprising. You should do this more often — let off steam and enjoy yourself.'

She tensed, confused by the fact that she was indeed enjoying herself. Her eyelids fluttered downwards to avoid meeting his probing gaze, and a little sigh escaped her lips. They were moving as one person, their bodies moulded together in perfect unison. This was the man she was determined to keep away from, yet the sensations coursing through her were overwhelming.

I must be crazy, she thought desperately, *it must be the champagne.* She tried to pull back, but he held her in a vice-like grip, thigh to thigh, the muscles of his chest flexing against her.

'Don't fight me, Gina.' His voice was husky in her ear. 'I always get what I want.'

She stopped dancing at once. What an idiot she was, reacting to his carefully devised stalking. He was not interested in her — the object of his desire was the Eastern. Here she went again, behaving like a vulnerable teenager where a man was concerned — and David had shown her how dangerous that could be.

'What's the matter?'

She shrugged. 'I want to sit down, I'm tired.'

His look left her in no doubt that he did not believe her, but 'OK,' was all he said.

The rest of the evening passed in a strange jumble of emotions for Gina.

She wanted so much to fend off her overbearing escort, yet found, in spite of herself, that he could be pleasant company. An attentive host, he never left her to her own devices, but made sure he introduced her to his many business acquaintances who popped over to their table to chat to him. He spoke intelligently on a broad range of subjects including the ballet, and did not hog the conversation, but listened attentively to the views of others.

'Such a nice man,' said Mrs Lindt when Jude was temporarily away from his seat, and Gina didn't wonder the woman was taken in. If he had not been a successful businessman, he would have made a good actor, she decided — witness the performance he was giving tonight of the reasonable, thinking woman's crumpet.

Only she knew his real ploy — to lull her into a false sense of security before making his strike to take over the Eastern.

When they left, just before midnight,

Mr Lindt made a feeble joke as he watched them get ready to depart, an envious sort of longing in his eyes.

'If you kiss Jude goodnight, he may turn into a handsome prince!'

Gina smiled politely. Had he got the wrong idea about them! Still, it just showed how well Jude had performed.

'More likely become a poisonous toad,' she replied with a smile, which made Mrs Lindt — who Gina suspected was shrewder than her husband — laugh.

The object of their mirth murmured softly, 'Ah, the Swan Princess has claws!'

So he knew her pseudonym. Well, that was no surprise; he was a businessman making a hostile takeover bid, and knowledge was power. It was plain he had found out as much as he could about her.

She made no objection this time when he opened the passenger door, but she pulled it shut quickly so he couldn't go into his seat belt routine again. Once she had fastened the clasp she looked up and saw he was laughing at her from the driver's seat, and she bristled. How did the wretched man always manage to make her feel at a disadvantage?

They drove in silence through the country lanes and on to the outskirts of Branchester. The car pulled up outside the ballet school, and she went to climb out, but his hand stopped hers on the handle. He looked at her for a while, and Gina felt her heart thumping against her velvet dress.

Slowly he leaned over her, sliding his arm along the back of her seat. She considered making an escape, but the moment when she could have done so passed, and then she was a prisoner to her own need. He drew her to him and she did not resist — she was overcome by an almost feverish desire for his kiss.

His mouth skimmed hers lightly, and she let out a small moan at the fire it caused to explode inside her. Such a small thing to provoke such a bewildering reaction! He became more demanding, forcing his lips upon hers, and, almost without realising she did so, she lifted her arms to reach behind his dark head and pull him nearer. Overtaken by a wildness she had not known she possessed, she responded eagerly.

'So beautiful,' he whispered, cupping her chin in his hand, 'and unawakened — like *Sleeping Beauty*.'

She felt as if she had been slapped, cold fingers of hurt clutching her heart. So David had been right — she was deficient in some all-important emotion most women had and that men wanted, and when they started to caress her, they discovered the fact.

Blindly she pushed Jude from her and stumbled out of the car.

She heard him open his door to follow, but he tripped, cursing loudly, and she was inside before he could reach her. She slammed and locked the front door, then leaned back on it as sanity returned.

Fool, fool! she castigated herself, *you knew all along he was only after one thing, and that certainly wasn't you! It's the Eastern he wants!*

She heard his car roar off out of the gravelled drive, and she shivered with apprehension. For all that he had been playing a part, Jude Alexander had not struck her as someone who would accept rejection lightly, and she feared what he might do as revenge.

Now it was all-out war . . . and with a dangerous man as her opponent.

4

In spite of her fears, the next few weeks proved happier ones for Gina than she had experienced for a long time.

At first she was nervous, jumping at shadows as if she expected Jude Alexander to materialise at every turn and demand to buy the company, but when he had not contacted her for a couple of weeks, the tension wore off and she was able to dismiss her feeling of unease.

Mr Lindt seemed to have had a change of heart, too, becoming unexpectedly helpful, not to mention generous, when she rang him with a plea for more time to start repaying the loan.

'That's all right.' He was quite avuncular over the phone. 'We'll leave the capital repayments until next year, so long as you keep up with the monthly interest.'

While he was being so amenable, Gina decided to ask about a further small loan to tide them over. She did not hold out much hope, but he answered, 'Of course, m'dear, no problem. We'll arrange an overdraft facility for you.'

He didn't mention how he thought she would be able to repay it, and she didn't like to ask. She was flying very close to the wind, and knew it, but still clung stubbornly to the belief they would break even by the end of the season.

'When shall I come in to sign the papers?'

'Oh, I'll contact you when they're drawn up.'

Only he had not done so yet, and she was not about to chase him over the fact.

Spring came suddenly and early, and she found her spirits rising with the bulbs that popped up in the parks and gardens. The old cherry tree by the terrace was covered in tiny white flowers, so delicate they looked like a fine lace, and when the cold East Anglian wind blew, the petals were scattered around like confetti.

Also carried on the wind were the sweet scents of those brave flowering shrubs which made up with their perfume for the insignificance of their blooms: the witch hazel, daphne and wintersweet. The sun shone brightly every day, the warm rays softening the worst of the wind's bite, and fluffy white clouds scudded across clear blue skies.

'Isn't it wonderful weather?' Gina was walking through Branchester's colourful open-air market with Madame Berthe, and gave a quick, unselfconscious pirouette to illustrate how good she felt.

The ballet mistress smiled her agreement. Praise be that it appeared Gina was returning to her old self again. She had lost the strained, haunted look she had carried around since *Karenina*, and was dancing a great deal better now that an apparent improved financial situation meant she no longer had to skip as many classes to worry about the books. It was almost as if she were mimicking the spring, coming out of a long, cold hibernation to make a fresh start — a rebirth.

'I'm glad you're not driving yourself as hard as you did.' Madame Berthe waited while Gina bought a bunch of violets from a stallholder. 'Someone needed to speak to James to make him see sense.'

'I don't think anyone has spoken to Dad — he hasn't had a lot to do with it. It appears Mr Lindt now realises we are a viable proposition, and has eased up on some of the restraints with which he initially boxed us in.'

The older woman raised her eyebrows questioningly at this statement, but made no comment.

'Simple flowers are the best.' Gina went on, inspecting her violets. 'I just hate wired bouquets, don't you?'

'I don't get many these days, but when I was dancing I preferred loose sheaths, yes.' Berthe smiled. 'By the way, which besotted fan sends you a dozen red roses every night?'

Gina looked uncomfortable. She was not certain sure who her secret admirer was, for the roses were never accompanied by a card, but she had a pretty good idea.

It annoyed her, for she was sure he was only doing it to put her at a disadvantage — she had not thanked him for that first bouquet, which she acknowledged had been rude of her, but she had been so preoccupied at the time it had quite slipped her mind when she next saw him. Now Jude was taunting her by dispatching roses without a name attached — or was he?

It would be just like him to torment her, but she had to admit that as he had made no attempt to contact her since the dinner-dance, it was a strange thing to do.

She supposed she could always phone up the florist and find out who ordered the flowers, but that might get back to him and she didn't want to draw attention to herself. No, best to let sleeping dogs lie.

She would not admit, even to herself, that she was scared of meeting Jude Alexander again — terrified of the emotions he had stirred up in her.

They wandered towards the theatre, and as they walked Gina found herself comparing the way she felt when dancing with Jude, to the no less exciting but emotionally very different night when she had met David Bryant . . .

* * *

It was at the end of the Eastern Ballet's three-week appearance under canvas at Battersea. Every year they put on a limited season in a circus tent just across the River Thames, as near to Covent Garden as a small company such as theirs was ever likely to get. She had been staying in digs with her parents at a flat in Lavender Hill, and, as always, they remained in London for a two-week break after the shows were completed.

'You can amuse yourself, can't you, Swan Princess?' her father had repeated every morning, and she had agreed she could. Usually her parents arranged lots of excursions and visits for them as a family to make up for the lack of time they were able to give to Gina the rest of the year, but on this occasion they had gone out a lot as a couple, leaving Gina to fend for herself.

She was surprised but not upset by this change in plans; she was nearly eighteen by then, and had learned independence and discipline from an early age. She was also secure in the knowledge of her parents' love.

James had arranged for her to go to the matinée of *Cinderella* at the London Coliseum. The British National Ballet was presenting a new version, and Gina particularly wanted to see it. She had an excellent seat, in the first row of the dress circle, and she leaned forward eagerly as the house lights dimmed.

'Ladies and gentlemen,' the announcer imparted the bad news, 'due to the indisposition of John Lambert, the part of the prince will be danced this afternoon by David Bryant.'

Gina was disappointed. John Lambert was one of her favourite dancers, and she had never heard of David Bryant — but from the moment of his first entrance, she was enthralled. He had a neat figure and a large jump, so unusual in British dancers, and his boyish smile and mobile face soon had the audience eating out of his hand.

That a lot of their goodwill was due to sympathy for a novice plucked out of obscurity at the last moment and doing his best to succeed, was lost on Gina. She was too young to understand, and the warmth of his reception coloured her opinion of his prowess as a dancer when she later pleaded his case to her father.

She had gone backstage after the final curtain call, hating herself for acting like a stage-struck adolescent, but unable to stop herself. Her name gained her entrance to his dressing-room, which was crowded with well-wishers, and at first he had seemed indifferent to her stammered congratulations. Feeling foolish and gauche, she had been about to make her retreat when a former member of the corps de ballet at the Eastern recognised her.

'Hello, Gina! What are you doing here? I thought your circus season was over.'

'It — it is,' Gina stammered. 'We're staying on as a family for the next fortnight.'

'David, do you know Gina George, daughter of the great James?' There was no irony in the introduction — James George was considered a national treasure in the ballet world.

'James George's daughter?' Until that moment, David had been engrossed in conversation with a shapely blonde, to whom Gina took an instant and irrational dislike, but once he heard her name, his eyes snapped to attention, and he turned all his attention and charm on her.

And I fell for it, she remembered with rancour, *what a little fool!*

'Is anything wrong, Gina?' Madame Berthe asked. They had reached the piece of waste ground behind the theatre, and the ballet mistress was watching her closely.

'No, no, just someone walking across my grave.' Mentally Gina pulled herself together. David was in the past — she would not spend her life looking backwards.

'I wonder what the new owner will do with this.' Madame Berthe indicated the estate agent's board on the overgrown site, which now had 'SOLD' pasted across it.

'As long as they don't block the entrance to our yard, I don't care what they do. Mum tried to buy this piece of land, you know, but she died before the negotiations got very far, and after *Karenina*, we couldn't afford it.'

Madame Berthe patted Gina's hand lovingly as they both remembered Marjory, and together they walked towards the theatre.

A queue of people was waiting at the

box office, and Gina gave a delighted smile of relief. Life was getting easier. The perfect spring weather was encouraging people to venture out again after the cold, hard winter, but the temperature was not so yet so high that they wanted to stay outdoors in pub gardens or at home barbecues. Now all the company needed was a long, wet summer!

* * *

Two hours later, tired and aching, Gina breathed a sigh of relief when James called a break.

'Can I have a word, please, Miss George?'

Gina recognised Stan's nasal whine, and turned irritably to face him. Was there no end to the man's petty grievances? Hardly a week went by without some new complaint, and she had begun to detect a definite feeling of antagonism towards her from the other stagehands. But what was she to do? She tried to accommodate Stan's requests to the best

94

of her ability, but still he was not satisfied.

'Yes, Stan?'

'The men were wondering how much you intended to pay them for the gala on Saturday.'

'Pay them? Oh, come on, Stan, it's for charity. None of us gets paid, you know that.'

'That's all very well for people who have high salaries to begin with,' Stan sniffed. 'They can afford it. We can't, and we want overtime rates.'

'It's impossible — '

'Then we'll black the theatre that evening.' He looked very pleased with himself as he stomped away.

Gina looked after him in horror. The annual April charity show was always sold out and attracted a lot of publicity for the company, as well as making much-needed funds for the local hospice. It would be very awkward if people turned up to find a dark theatre. But what could she do? If she tried to use others to do the stagehands' work she risked an escalation of the dispute and possible strike action. She shook her head in disbelief — would things ever go right for the Eastern?

She changed out of her practice clothes as quickly as she could — she had to get out into the fresh air and think. She dawdled disconsolately towards the river, stopping to buy a cheese roll from the wholefood bakery on the way. The area had improved immeasurably since Marjory George had bought the Little Theatre as the Roxy Cinema all those years ago, and while, happily, it had escaped the worst excesses of gentrification, it was certainly no longer considered a slum.

The low rents had attracted small, alternative-type businesses initially — a health food store, a vegetarian restaurant, an importer of ethnic jewellery — and as they had proved successful, others had moved in. There was a friendly village-y atmosphere among them all, which Gina hoped would never be lost.

The threat of redevelopment was

always hanging over them for although attractive, the buildings had no real architectural merit and now the location had come up in the world, builders were often casting greedy eyes in their direction. However, they always came up against the same problem; the position of the Little Theatre was such that it would have to be included in any demolition scheme, and the Georges had resolutely refused to sell.

'Bother!' Gina had intended to sit on the lone bench beside the river, and was annoyed to see someone sitting there already. Selfish, she knew, because that person had just as much right to be there as she, but she had wanted solitude.

It was only when she was almost on top of him she realised his identity — and by then it was too late to retreat, for he had noticed her.

'What a pleasant coincidence.' Jude Alexander rose at her approach. She had forgotten how melodious was his voice, and found herself admiring it anew, which annoyed her. She was no longer that same girl who could be deceived by outward appearances — David had seen to that — yet she was unwillingly aware of the fine tremors that raced through her body as he took her hand and she slumped haphazardly onto the seat, her trembling legs sagging beneath her.

He took in her pale colouring and distracted air.

'You don't look very happy.'

She ignored the enquiring tone in his voice and made a great play of unwrapping her roll. What was he doing in the area, anyway? It was hardly his part of town. She shot him a suspicious look.

As if reading her mind, he said, 'I've just managed to get tickets for your charity gala.'

She blushed, sure he had only told her so to prove his excellent credentials for being in the vicinity.

'Much good it will do you, I'm afraid.' She spoke without thinking to try and cover her embarrassment. 'The stagehands have blacked the performance.' She was unaware that when she spoke her despair broke through, and so missed the look of concern that flicked across his face. 'We'll have to cancel.'

'Are the men adamant? What's their problem?'

'They seem to be. They want to be paid, but all the proceeds go to charity and we can't absorb the expense ourselves.'

'Nor should you — it would set a bad precedent, and you mustn't give in to pressure. That's Stan's work, I suppose?'

She nodded, bristling slightly at the natural way he assumed he had the authority to advise her. She was reminded, too, of their first meeting, when he had suggested she was unable to stand up to Stan's demands. Well, she had stood up to them today — and look where that had got her.

'Hmm — you can't antagonise the men by using casual labour.' He saw the situation at once. 'What about another theatre?'

'It may have escaped your notice, but there is only one other theatre in Branchester — the Royal — and doubtless it will be otherwise engaged on a Saturday night!' She was being prickly and knew it, but it was a form of self-defence. The very nearness of him was making her tense, and she was trying to hide the fact, from him and herself.

'I didn't mean a professional theatre, I was thinking of a private one. Mine, actually.'

She was dumbfounded.

'You have your own theatre?'

'Yes, in the grounds of my home — Melrose House.'

Now she understood. She had heard of the place; it was a small estate, some ten miles outside Branchester. According to the local newspaper, it had been lovingly restored to its former glory over the last two years by its new owner. So that was Jude Alexander's doing — and it had a theatre.

Nevertheless, an amateur hall used for Red Cross fetes and shows by the Women's Institute, was hardly a suitable place to present a charity gala, and she said so.

He listened to her objections about safety curtains, emergency exits and fire alarms and then demolished them one by one.

'I've had the theatre done up to the highest standards,' he concluded, 'and every legal requirement has been met and more.'

'It's not just that,' she argued. 'How can we let the audience know about the change of venue? There's no time to advertise the fact.'

'No need. We'll lay on coaches to drive them there once they arrive at the Little.'

'I can't afford it — '

'I can.' She was about to refuse his offer, but he was too quick for her. 'Just call it my contribution to the hospice,' he said.

Very smoothly done, she thought, *he knows that while I might want to turn him down on my own behalf, I can hardly do so when a good cause will lose out.* She was stymied, and she knew it. She felt as if she was being hijacked, and the high-handed manner in which he was taking over infuriated her. And yet . . .

There was something enormously comforting in having all the cares lifted off her back — of being treated as if she needed protection. Sometimes the loneliness of her situation assailed her.

Not for her the close, loving relationship her parents had enjoyed — after David, she had determined never to put herself in such a position of vulnerability again. She might know she was cold and unattractive to men, but there was no need to open herself to the chance of others discovering her flaw.

It had been a terrible shock to find out from David just what she lacked — though when they first met, all had been wonderful and Gina could not have been happier . . .

* * *

'We're going to a disco later — would you like to join us?'

David had held onto her hand after shaking it, and when he smiled at her, she felt as if she were the only person in the room. She had accepted, of course, and over the next ten days had fallen head over heels in love with him. She was only seventeen and he had been her first boyfriend.

The evening before she was due to return to Branchester, he had invited her to a party at his flat. It had been a bitter-sweet occasion for her — she had been excited in the company of his sophisticated friends with their frenzied chatter and superior attitudes — but an awful sense of impending loss overshadowed everything.

'Come in the garden with me.' David had taken her by the arm and guided her outside. They sat down on the prickly grass under a tree, the sickly-sweet scent of the honeysuckle that rampaged up it all around them, and Gina thought, with the intensity of youth, that her heart would break.

'I can't bear to say goodbye!' she

gulped as he slipped his arm around her and kissed her lightly on the cheek.

'Then don't.' Seated, he was a good head taller than her, and he looked down at her with a bold expression. 'We don't have to part.'

'What do you mean?' she gasped. Her heart pounded with excitement — was he about to propose?

'Just that — I could come to Branchester.' He had seen her puzzled, faintly disappointed expression and hurried on. 'Look, isn't Anthony May retiring this year?'

She nodded. It was common knowledge in the dance world that their principal male dancer was leaving to take up the post of regisseur with a German ballet company.

'Well, then, the Eastern Ballet will be needing a new danseur noble.' He leapt to his feet and executed a perfect entrechat six, landing on one knee in front of her. 'Your father need look no further.'

His self-confidence took her breath

away. Anthony May was one of the finest dancers in England, who had chosen to dance with a small company like the Eastern because of his long association with James George. Adoring David though she did, Gina was not so blind that she imagined David to be in the same league. She had observed him perform four times since *Cinderella*, on each occasion in relatively minor roles, and she realised with the right training and presentation he could become a very competent dancer ... But the principal of a ballet company? Even loyalty could not make her agree he was ready for that yet.

'What about soloist?' she suggested tentatively, and was rewarded with a sulky stare.

'I'll soon be that with the National,' he said. 'The Eastern hasn't the same kind of kudos. No, it's principal or nothing.'

She bit her lip apprehensively, wondering what to do.

'Don't you think I'm good enough?'

he demanded, visibly angry.

'Yes, yes, of course you are!' Gina could not bear to feel he was cross with her, and her heart overruled her head. 'It's just . . . well . . . perhaps Dad would like someone a little older — more experienced than you — '

'He can give me the experience, don't you see? With James George presenting me — creating ballets for me — I'll get all the experience I need!'

Even then the naked ambition in his voice had not alerted her. She had agreed to ask her father — after all, in artistic matters relating to the Eastern Ballet, the final decision was his. She comforted herself that he would not employ David unless he thought he had talent.

She had approached her father with trepidation. One thing he had impressed upon his daughter was the need for quality, and she knew she was being less than honest when she pleaded David's cause. He was not ready for the great classics, but she closed her mind to the

106

fact and suggested his name.

'Hmm, I've seen him dance on a couple of occasions, Swan Princess, and he's not danseur noble material yet.'

She might have guessed James would have beaten her to it. With his usual equanimity he had not tried to influence her whirlwind friendship with David in any way, but it was just like him to have gone and checked out her young man.

'But he'd work very hard, and what with Anthony leaving — '

He pulled her to him, and gave her a huge bear hug, which was unusual, for he was not usually a demonstrative man.

'All right — if it's what you want, we'll have him. Anthony doesn't leave for a few months yet, so we'll have some time to train your David up.'

She beamed her thanks. She was delighted but also quite taken aback. She really had thought her father would refuse her request — he must see something in David's dancing she herself did not. She wondered how she had missed it, and decided she was so in love that she could see nothing but David the boyfriend when he was on stage, rather than David the dancer.

Her mother had not been so keen but, strangely for her, had not argued her case very strongly. She had looked pale and wan in London that season, Gina remembered.

'I must tie David down to a water-tight contract,' was all she had said, and that she hadn't done so, as was discovered after her car crash, was one of life's great mysteries. Normally Marjory could not be faulted where paperwork was concerned, and it was this rare lapse that had allowed David to walk away from the Eastern Ballet without a backward glance after the debacle of *Anna Karenina*.

And out of Gina's life.

She frowned. The irony of the situation was not lost on her; the man she had loved had cut and run, while the controlling Jude Alexander seemed determined to stay.

'We won't be able to get any scenery,' she said now. 'It's all stored under the stage at the Little, and the stagehands could turn funny if we tried to move it.'

Although she accepted his solution was sensible — indeed, the only one available — still she made excuses. His presence disturbed her in a way she could not explain, and she felt a nervous anticipation in his company.

'No problem. Yours will be like all other charity shows, I assume, a mish-mash of some of the most popular and showy pieces around?'

'Yes.' Once again she was startled by his knowledge of the ballet. It was true — galas tended to be collections of well-loved classical snippets, and were one of the few occasions when playing to the gallery was not frowned upon.

'Fine — I've got a neutral sort of back-cloth we can use, and a couple of flats. What about costumes?'

'Oh, that'll be all right. We keep all our costumes in store in the cellars at

Boundary Road. Mum had some sort of air filtration unit installed to stop them getting damp and mildewed.' She saw his sceptical look. 'It does work.' She defended her mother. 'The only problem is, it's full now, so goodness knows where we'll put any new ones we might get. We tried to buy the land behind the theatre to build a new wardrobe department among other things, but I see someone else has done so now.' She didn't admit it had been cost that had prevented their purchase.

He did not seem very interested, and changed the subject. 'Well, I guess the next thing is for you to come and inspect the theatre prior to committing yourself. Is tomorrow morning OK?'

'Yes, fine.'

'OK, I'll pick you up from Boundary Road at nine o'clock.' He rose and departed without giving her a chance to express her gratitude. Was it because he suspected the truth — that any such thanks would stick in her throat — that he departed so swiftly, thus saving her from having to say anything? She rather thought that was the case, but instead of feeling grateful to him for allowing her to save face, she was annoyed, irked that once more he had somehow managed to make her feel beholden to him.

She ate her roll in silence, analysing the strange drift her emotions were taking — one moment elated, the next moody and cross. It was only to be expected she would be wary of men after the tongue-lashing David had given her, but with Jude Alexander she was undergoing a totally new experience, and one, she had to admit, that tempted her as much as it frightened her.

What an idiot she was to be so susceptible to his autocratic interference — it was no use kidding herself he was doing any of this to make life easier for her, however comfortable the idea of being relieved of the burden. Surely she had learned that men never did anything for nothing?

She remembered how David had ingratiated himself with her for his own ends, and now Jude Alexander was doing the same thing. He wanted the Eastern, and he was only interested in helping her to further his own cause. Had she not sworn off all relationships once David had left her, bruised and broken in spirit, and vowed no man would ever control her again?

Then why was she weakening now?

It was true Jude's solution had been timely and welcome, but this feeling of relief — the desire for a shoulder to lean on — it showed her resolve was not as strong as it might be. She was convinced she was not really attracted to the man himself, it was just social conditioning that had defeated her momentarily into accepting the old adage that when life gets tough, the female of the species must turn to a mate for protection.

Well, she had done so once before, and had received vilification rather than support. It had taught her men were duplicitous and that it was far safer to remain independent.

And once this gala was over, she had every intention of becoming so again.

5

She awoke early the next morning with an odd feeling in her stomach that was a mixture of excitement and apprehension.

She had told her father about the gala's change of venue the previous evening. He had been saddened by the stagehands' action — like her he remembered the close, united front the Eastern had seen under Marjory — but seemed delighted by Jude's offer.

'It's very kind of him to help us,' he said and slipped her an enquiring glance. 'He seems a pleasant enough man.'

Oh, no, thought Gina, dismayed, *surely he's not falling for Jude's smooth line in patter?*

'He's only helping us to help himself,' she insisted. 'He's just waiting for the chance to pounce and stake his claim on the Eastern.'

James George backed down immediately.

'Well, if that's how you feel, Swan Princess . . .'

'It is!' She had shocked herself with her own vehemence. Was it because she now admitted that Jude Alexander had the power to make her respond to his touch — however unwillingly — that she was being so jumpy about what was purely a business excursion?

She didn't know. The only thing she was sure of was the fact that he was dangerous to her in some way — that if she let him get too close, she could get burned.

But he means nothing to me, she insisted, and as if to prove the point, she pulled on a pair of jeans that had seen better days and an old sweatshirt before tying her hair back into a severe bun. She would make no allowances for her femininity just because he was around.

The sound of a car crunching across

the gravel warned Gina of Jude's arrival, and she hurried outside to greet him.

'Good morning. Lovely day we have for it.' He took her by the elbow to guide her to the car, end although it was only the lightest of touches, she jumped back as if scalded. He said nothing, but his quizzical look showed he had identified her discomfort and was amused by it.

In the car she remained on edge, just waiting for him to bring the conversation round to his intended acquisition of the company. If he did so, she knew that today at least, because of his help over the gala, she would have to make a show of listening to him. He would be taking an unfair advantage, of course, but she doubted he would worry about that, and not for the first time she wished she were not in his debt.

Experience had taught her not to trust men, especially those with an ulterior motive for feigning friendship, and she would rather have had no

116

further contact at all with Jude Alexander.

Yet, strangely, he made no mention of the Eastern except in so much as it pertained to the present arrangements, and chatted in a friendly manner as they drove along. If he noticed her reticence, he made no comment on it, and she gradually relaxed, sinking back into the comfortable seat with the warm spring sun on her face, enjoying the drive in spite of herself.

'I haven't known this part of the world long,' he said as they sped towards the outskirts of the city, 'but I love it — don't you?'

Gina was taken aback by the warmth in his voice — it was the last thing she would have expected from such a tough businessman.

'I've never really thought about it,' she admitted, 'it's just home. But I'm always glad to get back after a foreign tour — I suppose because it's where my roots are and it gives me a feeling of security.'

'Lucky you.' There was no self-pity in his tone, but Gina got the impression he was speaking from the heart.

'I'm surprised you think so. I would've thought the bright lights of London would be more your scene.'

'Which just goes to show how deceptive appearances can be . . . I was brought up in north Kent,' he went on when it was clear Gina intended to make no reply. 'My father died when I was five and my mother had to go out to work to support us. She was a nurse and did night duty so she could look after me during the day. She felt, having lost my father so young, it was imperative I didn't get the impression she was deserting me too, so our landlady used to look after me at night and Mum would clean the house by way of payment. I don't know where she got the energy.'

He broke off, his eyes holding a faraway expression.

'She must be very proud of all you have done.'

'She didn't live to see it. The long hours and the struggle took their toll, and she had a heart attack when I was sixteen. I was devastated — I had sworn I'd drag us out of the poverty which I'd seen grind her down — and then she was gone before I got a chance.'

Gina, too, had lost her mother young, but she at least had the comfort of wonderful memories, and he did not.

'I'm sorry,' she said, 'and I do understand how you feel. I felt guiltier over the flop of *Anna Karenina* because Mum had died. I wanted to make it a success for her sake, as a memorial to her, and now I never can.'

'You think not? I wonder . . . ' He paused before continuing, 'Anyway, it's my understanding that the failure of the ballet was not your fault.'

She tensed. She did not want him to make excuses for her, but he didn't seem to notice.

'I know what you mean, though, I wanted to make up for all sacrifices my mother had made for me. She worked so hard — I only ever remember her with the yellow pallor and dark bags under her eyes that are the hallmarks of the perpetual night worker — and all the promises I made about holidays and rest came to nothing.'

Gina had not thought she would ever find herself feeling sympathy for the self-assured man sitting next to her.

She said, 'In the final analysis, I shouldn't think that was what was most important to her.'

'No,' he agreed, 'and being orphaned at an early age made me even more determined to get ahead. I had to succeed to keep faith with her, almost — and perhaps there's truth in the old maxim about having had to be really hungry before you can learn to win.'

Gina gave a little shiver as he spoke. Was there a warning there for her? Did he mean the reason she was failing with the Eastern was because it had been handed to her on a plate — so different from his own experience?

She wondered if Jude would later

regret showing her his vulnerable side; she knew she could not. It made him appear more human, and while it couldn't excuse his determined business tactics, at least it explained them.

They drove on in silence, and Gina enjoyed the brightness of the day. Some ten miles outside the city, they took a right turning off the main road and headed for the Newton Valley. The country road was narrow and muddy, with banks of primrose beneath the hedgerows and fat, sticky buds just bursting in the trees. Suddenly Jude made an indication left, and turned down a long avenue of pollard limes.

How the other half lives, thought Gina without rancour as they pulled up outside an Elizabethan manor house of warm red brick, with stepped gables and pediment windows. It was a family home rather than a stately one, and she wondered whether that was why Jude had bought it. He was a very eligible man, when all was said and done, and of an age when it might have been expected that his thoughts would turn to marriage. She would have thought there were any number of eager women who would be only too delighted to take on the task of chatelaine, and was startled to find the idea depressed her.

'Would you like a cup of tea before we begin?' he asked, and remembering that she had had no breakfast, Gina nodded her thanks and followed him indoors.

Inside, all was as welcoming as the exterior had promised, and Gina admired the oak panelling and sturdy Tudor furniture which graced the great hall and morning room. There were some fine paintings on display — she knew little about art but recognised they must be originals — and everywhere was a quiet calm and the smell of fresh wax polish.

'Do you spend a lot of time here?' she asked over tea, thinking what a crime it would be to leave such a lovely house unused.

'Yes, and I intend to spend more in the future. I'm moving the whole of my business operation up here from London.'

'Not to this house?' Gina was aghast. It would be criminal to spoil the perfect proportions by dividing up the rooms into offices.

'No, I have other plans for the business premises.' He dismissed her fears. 'But I've worked very hard for years and think it's about time I indulged myself. With the internet and electronic means of communication there really is no need for the company headquarters to stay in the City — so now all I have to do is persuade my staff they'll have a better life in East Anglia.'

She noted his supreme self-confidence that he would be able to encourage his entire work-force to decamp to an unknown part of the world. So she was not the only person whose life he was trying to control, she thought. It appeared he expected everyone to do his bidding.

'Has it occurred to you that they might not want to move, and might resent your overbearing interference in their lives?' she asked with asperity.

He met her antagonism with a mocking smile.

'Oh, yes — whatever you might like to believe, I don't ride rough-shod over my employees. I've arranged for them all to come down and spend a weekend in a hotel in Branchester and have a look around the area. Most of them feel it will be a wonderful opportunity to move here, houses are more affordable for one thing, and as a small office will have to remain in London, those that don't want to come won't be made redundant. My staff like working for me; we rarely have any industrial unrest.'

The jibe was not lost on her: the whole reason she was here with him was because her staff had threatened strike action, and there was no way she could deny it.

'Shall we go and see the theatre?' she said. 'I don't have much time.'

His look told her he knew it was an excuse, but he didn't contest her statement and took her out into the beautiful gardens at the rear of the house.

'This way.' They passed a seventeenth-century knot garden and an ancient yew hedge.

'Here.' He stepped through a break in the bushes and pointed ahead.

It looked like a large tithe barn, and although she had been expecting no better, Gina was disappointed. In spite of Jude's insistence that the interior had been modernised, she doubted he understood what was required from a professional theatre in general, and one where ballet was performed in particular.

The stage, especially, had to be good: smooth, with little or no rake and a good bounce to it.

She followed him down the path to the entrance, and blinked as she left the brilliant sunshine for the darkened auditorium.

'Voilà!' He turned on the lights, and she could detect the note of pride in his voice.

She could see why. It was quite delightful. The foyer was restrained and restful, but the auditorium proved to be a jewel-box of a place with red walls, red seats and carpets, gilt chandeliers and a plush red velvet curtain to complete the picture. She climbed up the steps to the stage and inspected the excellent equipment and lighting-board, before trying a few tentative steps out front. The stage felt like a dream, and she continued the adagio she was dancing, unconscious of Jude's studied observation.

'It's perfect,' she cried in delight. 'But why on earth have you spent so much money on a private, country house theatre?'

'You think it's a waste of money?'

'I think it's a waste of a theatre. It's much too beautiful to stand empty most of the time!'

He sauntered out to join her. 'I hope it won't be. It's my intention to hold recitals here — not for large groups, you understand, but for small companies like your own. Eventually I hope to develop a summer season of music and dance.'

'Including ballet?' She was interested.

'Yes, and opera, chamber music, jazz — you name it, I'll present it. I intend to let the audience picnic in the grounds during the interval, rather like Glyndebourne, but on a much smaller scale.'

'It sounds wonderful!' For once her excitement overcame her natural caution, and she gave him a wide smile. She didn't notice how he caught his breath, and she rushed on, 'The size is just right for the gala — nice and intimate, but not too snug.'

'Glad you approve. Have you time to see the rest of the place?'

She remembered who she was with.

'No, I don't think so.'

He sighed at her abrupt withdrawal.

'When are you going to stop fighting me, Gina?' His voice was raw, and he ran a finger lightly down her cheek. She flinched as a fierce spasm shot through her body, and she tried to pull away, but he caught her wrists and held her fast.

'I don't know what you're talking about — '

'I think you do. You treat me like a dangerous criminal most of the time. What do you think I'm going to do

— kidnap you and keep you prisoner?'

'No, I'm well aware you want something far more important than me — you want the Eastern!'

He kept his grip on one wrist, and with his other hand tilted her chin so she was forced to look at him.

'Do you really have such a low opinion of your own worth?'

She shrank back, terrified by his persistence. There were some things best kept private — things she did not want him to find out — she could not bear to see the undeniable admiration in his eyes turn to disgust . . .

She gasped. Admiration? What had made her imagine he would ever admire her? It was ridiculous, and dangerous, and she dismissed it from her brain at once.

'I save my low opinion for members of your sex,' she muttered. 'I speak from unpleasant experience.'

'But not much,' he returned, 'and David Bryant was hardly the man to give it to you.'

She staggered as if physically slapped. Really, he was insufferable!

But he had not finished. 'What did he do to you to make you shut yourself away from the mainstream like a clam?' and as her dumfounded expression mirrored her disbelief at what she had just heard, he added, 'I warned you I'd been asking around about the Eastern.'

'My private life has nothing to do with the company!'

'When it affects your performance, it has. Two years ago you were the great hope of the company, now you're called an also-ran. Oh, you still dance competently, but the fire has gone — it's all mechanical technique with no emotional depth.'

'Perhaps I was a child prodigy and now I'm all burned out!' She tried to sound flippant, but her tight, defensive expression spoke the truth.

'No, to burn takes passion, and you've long since denied yourself that pleasure.'

Her face turned ashen. So it was true

what David had said — for here was another man telling her she was passionless. Not only that, but her lack of it must be all too obvious to everyone. Hot tears filled her eyes, and she turned away quickly, and so did not see the sudden frown which creased his brow. She felt the slackening of his grip and took advantage to push him away and run off stage, determined he should not see her moment of weakness.

He caught up with her in the garden.

'I'd like to go now,' she said, clasping her hands behind her back so he should not see they were shaking.

'I'm sorry if mentioning David hurt you — '

'He was just a man I once knew.'

'And you don't like men very much at the moment, do you?'

It was gently said, but still she choked at his words. Why did men always have to let her know how undesirable her character was — how obvious the impression she gave of not liking them? She accepted it was true — what reason would they have for lying? But as there was nothing she could do about it, why did they have to rub it in?

'I was foolish once — I believed a man who told me he loved me.' She surprised herself as she admitted the fact. Usually nothing would induce her to talk about her experience. 'Now I know there's no way someone like David would be remotely attracted to me, and I'll never be stupid enough to believe anyone who says he loves me!'

'You can't lock up your heart and hide away the key forever.'

He said it kindly, and Gina was startled. How did he know that was the way she felt — that she had vowed never to trust a man again? The steel bands she had used to bind her emotions kept her safe, but they could not relieve the leaden ache of rejection.

'It's safer this way,' was all she said.

'Safe and sterile,' he told her, unforgivably.

Sterile, frigid, cold . . . was there no end to the names men would call her?

'I'm sure you'll be astounded to learn that not all women are just waiting for Mr Right to come along. I'm not, and I certainly don't intend to fall in love again.'

'You can't — you'd have to be able to love yourself first.'

She flushed, gripping the side of the car.

'I'd like to go,' she repeated without emotion.

'You'll have to get used to my blunt way of speaking.' He ignored her request. 'I'm looking forward to getting to know you better. I want to find out how a teenage Juliet becomes a twenty-year-old Queen of the Wilis.'

The allusion was not lost on her. Once, it was true, she had been that joyous young Italian — but love had not brought happiness for her any more than it had for Romeo and Juliet, and now she did indeed feel as stone-hearted as the cruel queen from *Giselle*, who demanded the ultimate punishment for a lover's infidelity.

She smiled at him without mirth.

'And like all men, you can't believe how very resistible your sex can be.'

Laughing, he leaned forward to pat her playfully — condescendingly, she thought — on the head.

'Is that why you drag your hair back into that ghastly bun?' he demanded. 'To make yourself less attractive to resistible men?'

She trembled at his touch, her scalp tingling as if she had received an electric shock.

'Dancers need to wear their hair tied back neatly.' She spoke nothing but the truth. 'We have to keep it out of our eyes for class, and when you've had something drummed into you all your life, it ends up as second nature.'

'A shame,' was all he said, but his eyes, as he swept them over her, spoke volumes. 'You're shivering.'

'I'm cold!' she snapped back, knowing the bright sunshine proved her a liar. In reality she felt as if she were on fire, every muscle in her body stretched with an unbearable tension under his scrutiny.

She did not kid herself that Jude Alexander found her desirable — she had allowed herself the pleasure of the belief that a man had wanted her once before, and had paid a heavy price for such foolishness. Men might call her the Swan Princess, and admire her as that untouchable queen of the ballet, but in real life she left them cold.

'I have some work to do here.' He seemed to lose interest in taunting her. 'I'll get someone to run you home.'

'Thank you.' In reality she wanted to tell him what he could do with his lift.

'Your smile is all the thanks I need.' He gave a mock bow, the irony in his voice showing he understood her dilemma.

Gina gritted her teeth and waited while he arranged for his driver to run her to the ballet school. The journey was an uncomfortable one, as a wild jumble of emotions welled up inside her.

In spite of the strange effect his presence had on her, she refused to be taken in by Jude Alexander's smooth talking and elegant ways. He might present the façade of an engaging, reasonable man, but she recognised another side to him — a determination to get what he wanted which he could never completely hide, and which reminded her of David's ruthless exploitation. She was sure Jude was trying to submerge this aggressive streak to lull her into a false sense of security so that she would accept his offer of a partnership — he must have worked out that her previous experience with David meant she would not succumb to mere love-making. Thank heavens she was immune to his advances!

Or was she? She was troubled that she seemed unable to control her feelings when Jude was around. Why was she so uneasy in his company? It was something she couldn't explain.

She didn't trust him, didn't approve of his business methods and the way he was hassling her father, certainly didn't fancy him . . . and yet she had to admit that she reacted to his presence with a frisson of sensation that set her nerves jangling. She suspected it was some sort of self-defence mechanism following her abortive affair with David — an unconscious warning of how vulnerable she would be if she let another man get close to her — but it was an unfamiliar phenomenon and had caught her off guard. She liked to feel she was in total control of her emotions, and was annoyed to discover Jude's macho posturing could so disturb her.

★   ★   ★

Once back at the ballet school, she hurried to pull on her practice clothes for class — tights, leotard, knitted crossover and leg-warmers, and joined the throng of people heading for the Garden Studio.

'Good, Gina, but softer, a little gentler . . . '

Madame Berthe watched as Gina

feverishly threw herself into the lesson. *Almost as if she's punishing herself*, the woman thought, little knowing how near the mark her assessment was.

Gina was forcing her body to the very edge of endurance — her turn-out more pronounced, her extensions far longer, her positions more developed than even the high standards called for by the ballet mistress. She drove herself without mercy, as if to prove that while her emotions might hot obey her, her body was her own tool, to be used as she and not another saw fit.

She remembered the fable of the tarantella, that wild Neapolitan dance whose frenzied abandonment arose out of the belief that following the bite of a deadly tarantula, the poison could be danced out of one's system to save one's life.

In some strange way, that was how she felt — as if by forcing her body to the point of exhaustion she could rid it of all trace of Jude Alexander, whose potency seemed as dangerous as any spider's bite.

'That is the old Gina I knew!' Madame Berthe complimented her. 'You have regained your zest for life.'

Had she? As she left the studio, hot and aching, she wondered what had made the change, and realised with a start that it was Jude's blunt critique of her dancing that had spurred her on to try harder. She supposed she ought to feel grateful to him, but she didn't; rather, she resented the way he had invaded her life and left her feeling ill at ease with herself.

She stripped off in the changing rooms and took a shower, soaping herself fiercely, as if by so doing she could wash away the memory of the man and his all-encompassing aura.

Dressed in jeans and a T-shirt, she made her way to the garden flat, and as she crossed the threshold, she heard voices on the terrace. Her father had company; she made to join him until the deep liquid tones reached her ears, and then the realisation of the identity of his visitor caused the hair at the back of her neck to prickle.

She knew she should make her presence known or withdraw, but she waited too long, and the moment when she could have joined them passed, yet she could not drag herself away.

'So you think with a new partner, it would all work out?' her father asked.

'Yes,' the familiar dark brown voice rumbled. 'Gina won't like the idea at first, of course, but she'll come round to it.'

Gina stood as if rooted to the spot. It sounded as if her father and Jude Alexander were considering a partnership without any reference to her! She ought to have realised Jude might approach James direct if she refused his offer, especially after he had accused her of trying to run her father's life.

The effrontery of the man, to say she would come round to the idea — as if she were a dog that could be won over by patting! His arrogance took her breath away. But what upset her most of all was the hole-in-the-wall way she had found out about it. She could not — would not — blame her father, he never would have encouraged such a notion himself; she had no doubt Jude had been badgering him, working on James' gentle nature to get his own way.

Only now she knew — and she intended to fight him with every weapon she had. The problem was, how did she bring up the subject when she was not even meant to know about the deal? She could just imagine Jude's reaction if he found out she had been eavesdropping, and she refused to give him another opportunity to put her down . . . but how else could she bring up the question of a partnership?

A chair scraping on the terrace as someone stood up interrupted her reverie, and she realised Jude was leaving. She darted behind the open door and watched through the crack as her father led his visitor out. Her heart was thumping so loudly she was sure she would be heard — how shaming to be discovered spying by that superior being — but they went past without detecting her. She slipped out of her hiding place and managed to meet her father in the corridor upon his return, giving the impression she had just arrived.

'Hello, Swan Princess.' He smiled. 'What did you think of Melrose Theatre?'

'It's beautiful,' she admitted, 'but I forgot to arrange when we'd do the run-through or see to the lighting — '

'That's all right, Jude's been here discussing the whole thing with me, and we've organised it all. You just missed him.'

She feigned surprise. 'Oh? Did he have anything interesting to suggest?'

James George did not bat an eyelid.

'Not really, just that he thought the best time for a run through would be late afternoon on Saturday, and I agreed.'

Gina nodded. So her father did not intend to tell her Jude had been trying to persuade him to accept the offer. She wondered why James should want to protect him. Perhaps it was Jude's

141

suggestion — after all, the businessman was well aware of her opinion of the deal, and it could be that he was hoping to get her father to agree without reference to her.

Or perhaps it was simply that the proposition did not appeal to James, indeed, meant so little to him that he didn't think it worth mentioning? She just prayed his silence did not indicate he had accepted the offer and was too nervous of her reaction to tell her.

'What about the stagehands?'

This is ridiculous, she thought — *here I am politely making small talk with Dad, talking around the one subject that really interests me.*

'Apparently Jude has an arrangement with the local amateur dramatics society. They crew his productions in return, for free use of his theatre for theirs. He was surprised you hadn't asked.'

'Really?' She tried to make her voice sound neutral, not wanting her father to hear her fury. Trust Jude to point out how remiss she had been! Foolishly she had given him another stick with which to beat her, for she was sure he would say that if she were running the Eastern Ballet properly, she wouldn't have overlooked such details. It was, after all, only what David had said.

Exactly as Jude had just done.

James appeared not to have noted anything odd as his daughter spoke, and he continued calmly, 'He says they are experienced and good, and I don't think he's a man who gives praise lightly.'

'No,' she agreed. 'I wouldn't have thought so either.' She recalled his criticism of her dancing, and knew he would not.

Was it true what he had said — that she was only able to interpret a role on an intellectual and not an emotional level, and that she tried to make up for the fact with showy athleticism? She didn't know any more — that she doubted herself both privately and professionally these days was yet another legacy from David. But she did believe in the Eastern, and was sure it should retain its independence if it was to survive as an artistically innovative company.

'And I won't let you destroy it!' When she was alone in her room, she spoke aloud to an imaginary Jude Alexander in the mirror.

The fierceness of her own expression startled her, and she realised with surprise just how much she feared him and what he could do to the company. She intended to fight him, but knew it would be a hard battle — and she didn't relish crossing swords with such a seasoned campaigner.

6

'Isn't he gorgeous?' Amelia Pierce was the youngest member of the Eastern Ballet Company, having joined the corps de ballet straight from school the previous July, and was still very excited by her new career.

She was a good dancer but not an exceptional one; she lacked the necessary intelligence to be really first class. Now her pleasant, rather vacant face was smiling stupidly at the scene in front of her, and she nudged Gina, who was sitting beside her, under the spreading canopy of a towering cedar tree, to try and get a response.

'Don't you think he's gorgeous?' she gawped, and Gina followed her view reluctantly.

Jude Alexander was bending over a wooden picnic table, one foot on the bench casually supporting his weight,

145

elbow on knee, as he regaled the laughing girl sitting opposite with his stories. She was one of the backstage crew, a member of the Newton Amateur Dramatic Society, and it was obvious she was enjoying the attentions of such an intensely masculine man. Her eyelids fluttered coyly, her pretty face set into lines calculated to please.

Poor thing, thought Gina, *little does she know what she's unleashing*. For Jude put her in mind of nothing so much as a wild animal, carefully tamed but never domesticated, who was just waiting to shake off the constraints of civilisation and pounce. His face moved closer to the girl, and Gina experienced a rush of illogical irritation, though whether against him or his enthralled audience, she couldn't say.

'He's OK if you like that kind of thing, I suppose,' she allowed, breaking off as the brooding face turned to stare at her for a moment, black eyes taunting as if he knew she had been talking about him and what she had said.

She glared back, refusing to be intimidated by his lazy smile, and inwardly railing against fate that had made him attend the dress rehearsal.

She had heard no more about a partnership since his visit to Boundary Road, and had hoped that meant her father was against the idea, but then Jude had turned up at the run-through looking remarkably pleased with himself, and she began to worry again.

She supposed he had every right to be there — it was his theatre, after all — but she resented the way he marched around with such familiarity that he might already have been a partner in the company. She ignored him, backing off whenever he looked as if he might come her way, and although she could tell from the cynical curve of his mouth that he understood what she was doing and was amused by the gambit, she was satisfied it was the best way to avoid him.

He stared on uninterrupted, and at last she dropped her eyes. *Conceited idiot*, she thought, but her body was trembling.

When she felt it safe to do so, she stole another look at him and noted he was once more firmly ensconced with the lovely stagehand. He held her fingers lightly as he spoke. Gina, mildly annoyed, wished he would leave the girl alone.

She knew her face had betrayed her feelings when he flashed her a look of pure triumph. Typical man! He was so vain he had read her annoyance as being directed against his actual canoodling with the girl, not against his chauvinistic attitude.

'I'm going indoors,' she told Amelia crossly, even though she didn't really want to leave the unseasonably strong sunshine for the gloom of the auditorium. She got up to leave and felt rather than saw Jude's eyes boring into her.

She was glad to make her escape into the shadowy theatre. All was quiet — most people were taking advantage of Jude's hospitality and eating the tea he had provided on the lawn after the final run-through. She entered her dressing-room, the most glamorous one she had ever had, and sat at the dressing-table, trying to compose her thoughts and wondering why she should feel so nervous when everything was going so well.

The run-through had gone like clockwork — the scenery Jude had provided was exactly what they needed, and the small orchestra had pronounced the acoustics excellent. They had no problems with the costumes — indeed Joan Hardy, the wardrobe mistress, had ignored Stan's directive and come out to help.

'Nasty, interfering little man!' she had sniffed. 'Don't know why the others listen to him. I've never given in to bullies, and don't intend to start now.'

Gina had smiled non-committally, not wanting her opinion of his behaviour to get back to Stan and cause more trouble, but secretly she agreed wholeheartedly.

'What a gem!' Her father had fallen

in love with the theatre at first sight, and Gina was disturbed to hear him discussing dates for future appearances with Jude. She would have to cancel those at the first opportunity — nice though the theatre was, the last thing she wanted was to dance there regularly with the chance of bumping into the disturbing Mr Alexander.

For somehow he seemed to have been able to get under her skin, invading her thoughts and attacking her equilibrium. This afternoon she had been tensely conscious of him watching her performance, and had had to arm herself against his presence. She could not understand it; she had determined never to allow a man to threaten her peace again, yet Jude Alexander seemed to have successfully pierced her shell.

She supposed it was because the situation was so like that with David. In fact, had it not been for his masterly tuition in the art of using someone, she might have fallen for Jude's attempt . . . and instinctively she knew he would be a far more dangerous proposition than the ballet dancer had been.

* * *

Once he had joined the company, David had wanted her with him all the time, so she had seen him every day. She danced with him, watched while Madame Berthe and her father encouraged and developed him, and, in their rare free time together, went out with him.

He was kind and gentle at first, eager to get into her father's good books, and never tried to take advantage of her innocence. Seven years older than she, he appeared to her both sophisticated and mature, and she had had no defence against his flattery and lies.

Rarely, he let the mask slip and exposed his sullen, petulant side — as had happened over the casting for *Anna Karenina*.

'I want to play the main role.'

James George had intended to create

151

the part of Vronsky, Anna's lover, for his old friend Anthony May, a fitting final tribute to a fine artist. David was furious when he heard, having banked on the part being his. He turned on Gina and berated her soundly for her disloyalty.

'But David,' she pleaded in vain, 'it's got nothing to do with me.'

'Don't give me that!' he spat out his reply. 'Your father would do anything for you. If you asked him, Vronsky would be mine!'

However she had not had to, because May himself had stood down.

'No, my dear boy.' He had waved aside all objections from James. 'It's a young man's part. Let the boy have it — he'll be OK as long as Alicia is there to control him.'

So David got what he wanted — and by way of a thank you, proposed to Gina.

'You're too young,' her mother had said. She looked distracted and worried these days — the new ballet was obviously causing some problems, Gina thought — but Marjory did not withhold her blessing.

'Are you sure it's what you want, Swan Princess?' Her father seemed sad.

'Oh, yes, Dad!' By then David had managed to convince her he was as wildly in love with her as she was with him. 'And don't worry, you won't be losing a daughter, just gaining an exceptional premier danseur!'

Two days later James George lost his wife.

It was a dreadful time. Having been such a close-knit family, the grief of husband and daughter was immense. David had proved less than supportive.

'What about *Karenina?* Will it still go ahead?'

Gina had nodded dumbly, too grief-stricken to diagnose his indifference to her suffering for what it was. But she had been brought up on the old theatrical saying *The show must go on*, and never doubted for a minute that it would.

★ ★ ★

Just as now, with the gala for the hospice . . . Suddenly she felt stifled, the heat in the dressing-room seemed to her to be overpowering in spite of the open window. She had to get out — to go for a walk and clear her head.

She slipped out of the stage door and headed for the distant woods, pausing only to peep through a gap in the yew hedge to place Jude. She did not want to run into him accidentally on her travels, but he was no longer there. The picnic bench was empty.

Wherever he was, she was sure he was not alone, and was dismayed by the slightly sick feeling the knowledge gave her.

She paced unseeing through the manicured lawns and herbaceous borders, striding quickly as if to put as great a distance as possible between herself and the house in the fastest possible time.

She came to the wild part of the

garden, its untouched beauty calming her ragged nerves, and she slowed to a more natural pace. The sun was sinking lower in the sky and the shadows lengthening, and she found a kind of peace as she tramped on through the leaf mould and tightly curled emerging fronds of bracken under the whispering trees. The noises of the forest — rustlings and cracking of twigs, great beatings of wings, squeaks and squeals and the pure, wet notes of bird song — charmed her, and the damp, rich smell of the earth permeated her very being, making her feel at one with nature.

Her footsteps were light and her tread noiseless, so she came upon him without advertising her approach. A sudden noise in the bushes alerted her, just as a twig snapped under her foot. She turned, eyes wide, just in time to see his figure silhouetted against the skyline.

The suddenness of his appearance startled her and she stumbled, only saving herself from falling by grabbing on to the nearest tree.

'Are you all right? You haven't twisted your ankle or anything?' Jude strode towards her. 'Haven't you been taught to take more care when walking on uneven ground?'

'Of course. Dancers are always wary of injury.' She bristled. 'I know some who won't do anything that might jeopardise their career, but Mum and Dad brought me up to accept nothing in life is risk-free and they allowed me the luxury of having as normal a life as they could. They let me go ice-skating with schoolfriends, even though Madame Berthe frowned on it, and they certainly didn't say I couldn't walk through the woods!'

He stood on a bank just ahead of her, the added inches making him appear like a giant. She could not see his face clearly, the bright sun shining directly behind him causing her eyes to water, but she made out the clothes he had been wearing earlier — dark green corduroys and a hacking jacket — and what she privately called his 'superior voice' was all too familiar.

He strode towards her. 'I wouldn't have let you come up here, anyway,' he said. 'You do realise you are trespassing? I offered you the use of my theatre, not the freedom of the grounds!'

The scream of some small woodland animal startled her again, and she jumped visibly. In one fluid movement, Jude was at her side, arm encircling her waist.

'Relax . . . ' His firm voice was steadying. 'There's nothing to be afraid of.'

She pulled away — the danger she feared was not so much from woodland wildlife as from him — but even as she struggled free, his hand shot out and pulled her to him fiercely. He misjudged his strength and her light weight and she was catapulted into his firm, warm chest, where she was startled to discover that his very nearness set her heart somersaulting alarmingly.

She had to admit she found the rock-like support comforting, and almost wished she could just stay there as she swayed slightly, a mixture of fatigue and longing overtaking her.

As if sensing her retreat, Jude enfolded her slight frame, rocking her gently in his arms. The effect on her was electrifying: her body sparked alive off his until she came to a new awareness, experiencing everything on a deeper level. He murmured in her ear, his liquid tones steadying her shattered nerves. She buried her face in the stuff of his jacket, smelling a mixture of leather, aftershave and a more natural odour which she could distinguish as his — human and exciting.

At last he eased her gently backwards, lifting her chin to look at him. With his finger he traced a pattern around the line of her jaw to her lips, where he paused for a moment to inspect her.

'Such a perfect mouth on such an innocent face,' he said. The words made Gina stiffen with the memory of pain and rejection. But he appeared not to notice, and bent to kiss her.

What's happening to me? she thought, panic rising. She, who always kept her emotions on such a tight rein, was experiencing the tantalising flames of desire.

Or was she? She remembered David's taunting words and knew it could not be so — he had told her such fire was beyond her. Soon her responses would give her away, and Jude too would know about her sad deficiencies as a woman.

'No, you must stop!'

His eyes blinked open. The pared lines of his face were strained as he gave her a quizzical look.

'Why?' he coaxed. 'You like it, your response makes that plain. Why are you so agitated?'

'I have to go — '

She stumbled away, trying to make sense of her fevered thoughts. It was only when she was back in front of her dressing-table and reviewing the situation that she realised how dangerous it could become.

Jude had said he could teach her many things; she was sure he could, but she doubted love was one of them. He was clearly a man well-versed in the ways of women, and could read her body language with no difficulty at all. Given her usual steely control, her mindless abandonment to his kiss would not have gone unnoticed.

She wondered how long it would be before he used the knowledge of her weakness to his own advantage. In her experience, men only formed relationships with her to forward designs of their own, and Jude had made clear what he wanted — the Eastern or nothing.

She looked at herself in the mirror and noted the flushed cheeks and swollen lips.

'I'll have to give him a wide berth,' she told her reflection. It would not be difficult once the gala was over; after all, she had been doing so for a different reason since they first met. Subconsciously she must have been aware of his attraction even then, which would account for the distrust she had always had of him.

She sighed as she came face to face with her Achilles heel: in the past she had tried to explain away the electrifying effect Jude had upon her, but now she had to admit she had a burning desire to know him better.

Forewarned is forearmed, she told herself sternly. She knew what Jude wanted.

★ ★ ★

It had been different with David — he had given her no reason to distrust him, though things had been difficult after Marjory's death.

'I don't understand it — Mum left a mountain of unfinished paperwork,' she told him after the funeral, when she stepped temporarily into Marjory's shoes. But he seemed only interested in the new ballet, and became annoyed when she wasn't around to help him.

'Where have you been?' he demanded.

'Trying to clear the backlog,' she

replied, but didn't burden him with the thousand and one other jobs engendered by the creation of a new ballet and which her mother had normally undertaken.

Then, three days before the opening night, Alicia Allen had pulled a muscle and had to withdraw from the production.

'You'll have to go on, Swan Princess.'

Gina was the official understudy, but she knew her dancing was not of the same calibre. Indeed, there had been little time for second cast rehearsals, and she had learned most of the part while watching her beloved David working with Alicia.

'Dad, I can't! Alicia is the only true prima ballerina of the company.'

'You were fine when I danced with you,' James said, for Gina had never even partnered David in the role before Alicia's mishap: her father had danced the part of Vronsky during understudy rehearsals. 'Just do your best.'

However her best had not been good

enough. Used to James's selfless habit of supporting ballerinas to show off their best points rather than pushing himself to the fore, she was to find David's way very different.

The day of the première dawned, and Gina awoke nervous but excited. She had learned the part in record time, and was confident that technically, at least, she would give a good performance.

The problem was, she had had no time to spend on artistic interpretation, and she knew that a great part of the ballet depended on Anna's emotional turmoil. Still, she told herself, she loved David just as Anna had loved Vronsky, and she hoped that fact, coupled with understanding partnering from her fiancé, would enable her to give a realistic portrait of the passionate Anna.

'That was good, Swan Princess!' James was waiting in the wings as she came off after the first act, tired but exhilarated. The scene, with Anthony May as Anna's husband, had gone well.

Like the premier danseur noble he was, Anthony had presented his ballerina so she was seen to the best possible advantage, and Gina's confidence had grown under his careful handling.

It was only when she started to dance with David in Act Two that things began to go wrong. Initially she was unable to work out what the matter was. Where in rehearsal Vronsky had been loving and supportive, David's interpretation on stage seemed to have changed with his new partner, and now he depicted him as crass and showy, with an unfortunate propensity for pushing himself to the forefront and upstaging everyone else. It was almost as if Vronsky was not so much in love with Anna, as with himself.

The applause at the end of their first pas de deux was tepid. Audiences used to the creative innovations of James George were clearly disappointed thus far, and Gina hoped their opinions would change after the interval.

Her father was speaking to David in

the wings, pointing urgently. She saw David's face — beaded with perspiration after his performance — flush to an angry red before he turned and walked away.

After that, it went steadily downhill. She felt herself sinking into a quagmire not of her making. David's performance grew more ostentatious, dazzling pyrotechnics replacing any attempt at artistic truth. Gina sensed they were losing the audience; that unique experience of energy crossing the footlights to ignite a strong emotional reaction — an invisible bond between those on stage and those in front of it — was missing.

The polite applause at the final curtain confirmed her worst fears. When James George came to take his bow, he looked shell-shocked.

'I have something to say to that young man!' Anthony May was simmering with rage. 'What on earth did he think he was doing?'

But with his usual instinct for self-preservation, David managed to slip away. Gina followed him, anxious to console him, and instead had learned a dreadful truth . . .

★ ★ ★

The half-hour call broke into her reminiscence, and she reached for her headdress. She felt him watching her, and whirled around.

'Thought about what I said?' Jude asked.

In her confusion she dropped the floral circlet. They both made a grab for it, but it was his hand that closed around it as they crouched, face to face, inches from each other. Slowly they rose, her hazel eyes wide with apprehension, his daring her to be the first to look away.

'Let me,' he ordered as they regained their full heights, his voice husky. He guided her back to her seat in front of the mirror, and placed the floral Alice band in place. Then, without pause, he bent to nibble her smooth neck. Unable to stop herself, she turned to meet his lips with hers.

'Gina, can I borrow your panstick?' Amelia bounced in through the open door. 'So sorry. I didn't realise you were engaged!' The double meaning suddenly hit her and she roared with laughter, before taking the proffered make-up and dashing out again.

'Is she a gossip?' Jude asked.

'And how!' Gina pulled a horrified face. 'She'll have us wedded, bedded and all the children named by the end of the performance.'

'Give the company something to talk about.'

But she was not amused. He might find the idea of a fictitious love affair funny, but she had suffered once before, acting out a romance in front of an interested audience, and although no one had been unkind to her about the outcome, she had heard the hushed whispers which called her naïve for believing David's lies.

His unbridled ambition had been

obvious to others even if she had missed the tell-tale signs. She did not want to give more fuel to wagging tongues; to fall for one unscrupulous man was understandable, but if she repeated the exercise the gossips would find it inexcusable. It would lay her open to much speculative chit-chat.

'I'll put her straight on the facts and make sure she keeps her mouth shut.' Gina backed away from him. 'Don't worry.'

'I shan't.' He moved closer and she recoiled. 'Gina, don't shut me out like this! You know there's something special between us — '

'I know there's something special you're after! I've told you before, the Eastern is not for sale!'

His mouth hardened into a straight line.

'Is that what you think this is all about?' he demanded. 'Gina, I'm no David — I don't form relationships to get my own way. Let's get one thing straight, I am not trying to seduce you to can get my hands on your father's company. I want 'in', yes, but I wouldn't stoop to that kind of method and resent you suggesting I would.'

'I'm sorry.' She was still not sure she could believe what he said. 'It's just that after David — '

'Please, don't compare me to him!' Jude's top lip curled with distaste. 'David was a man with his eye on the main chance, he only wanted to take, whereas I want to give as well. Both professionally and personally.'

'I want to believe you, but how can I be sure?'

'You can't.' His voice was brutal. 'You have to take a chance like everyone else.'

'The price is too high — '

'Coward.' He showed her no mercy. 'I called you that once before, but I was beginning to hope I was wrong.'

'I'm not a coward!' But secretly she feared she was. She didnt want to lay herself open to more pain and sorrow.

'Yes, you are. I don't deny David treated you badly, but you're simply prolonging the agony by hugging that hurt to yourself and using it as a shield whenever anyone tries to get close. Don't let one bad experience cloud your whole view of men — we're not all cheats, you know.'

She bit her lip. She so wanted to believe him, and yet . . .

'What about the Eastern?' She had to know. 'Why do you want it?'

He answered no more satisfactorily than he had the first time she had asked.

'I want to diversify into a new field. Also, the Eastern is just the type of company I could present here at Melrose House.' His smile was open and friendly, but she wondered why he had not mentioned Melrose House before. She still had the impression he was hiding something.

'How do I know it's me and not the ballet company you want?'

'Gina, how many times do I have to tell you I'm not David? I'm a different person with different — hopefully better

— values.' He squatted on his haunches to be level with her seated frame. 'I tell you what,' he said, 'if you are so sure this is all part of some Machiavellian plot, I've got a suggestion that may appeal to you. I'll drop all idea of becoming a partner in the company until I'm actually asked to do so, if you'll stop treating me like something nasty that the cat's just dragged in, and let me have a fair chance. We'll get to know each other and become friends and see if we want to take it further, OK?'

She considered his offer carefully. It was a sensible compromise — he would have time to prove his good intentions, she to learn to trust again — but would he keep to his side of the bargain? What if this was just a trick to get her to drop her defences? He could take over the Eastern tomorrow if she once dropped her guard. She should not gamble with the company ... yet she knew she could not bear to let him go.

'Do you agree?' he asked, urgency in his voice.

'OK, I agree. I won't prejudge you if you'll put your blueprint for the Eastern on hold.'

'Until I'm invited to become a partner,' he prompted. She nodded, secure in the knowledge that such an agreement made the decision hers.

'You'd better go. I have to finish getting ready.'

'Yes, I've got to change. By the way, what is the name of the piece you're dancing?'

'The pas de deux from *Flower Festival At Genzano*.'

He paused at the door and gave a wicked grin.

'I didn't think you liked flowers — at least, not red roses.'

She had the grace to blush.

'If that remark means you are the secret dispatcher of my nightly bouquets, please accept my thanks. But I'm no mind reader, and without a card, it was impossible to guess who sent them.'

He nodded, but she knew he didn't

believe her. It wasn't as if she had admirers queuing round the block with floral tributes!

'Good luck, or should I say 'break a leg'?'

'Probably not to a dancer.' She smiled, and then he was gone.

Securing the headdress in place with an armoury of hair pins, she looked in the mirror and the young lover from August Bournonville's most perfect ballet smiled back. It seemed to her there was a change in her appearance since she last danced it. She could detect a softening around her mouth and a general relaxation of the tension in her face, but it was her eyes that told the real tale. Radiantly bright, pupils dilated with happiness, they mirrored the giddying torment she was feeling.

Long-ago admonishments from her mother rose to taunt her: *You're getting over-excited, Gina, it'll end in tears.* But just as the child then had been mindless of the warning, so the young woman now was powerless to resist.

No longer could she sit on the sidelines of life, she had to partake of its wonders herself, and if she was hurt — well, at least the pain would prove she was alive.

7

'Plié . . . jeté . . . pas de bourrée over . . . now travel — travel on those jumps.'

Madame Berthe beat her cane on the floor in time to the piano accompaniment, and Gina finished the enchainment with a flourish, before walking to the side of the studio and collapsing over the barre. She was physically exhausted, sweat pouring from her brow as she followed the dancer's ceaseless quest for perfection, but strangely enough, since she had called a truce with Jude Alexander, she had felt more relaxed generally than she had for the past eighteen months.

She knew why, of course. Since David had left her, she had carried around a huge burden of guilt and sorrow, not only for the failure of *Karenina*, but also for her failings as a woman. She had long ago come to accept that David had never loved her; what had been harder to bear was the belief that no man ever would.

Up until his harsh accusations she had assumed that alongside her career, her life would take the normal course of marriage and motherhood. When she discovered that was not to be a way open to her, she had flung herself into running the company, as if ledgers and cash flow sheets could take the place of human relationships.

But they couldn't, and yet she had been unable to move on — David had seen to that.

The party after the opening of *Karenina* was understandably subdued, and only he seemed unaffected by the atmosphere. He was drinking heavily, and was quite unrepentant about his performance.

'I don't believe in hiding my light under a bushel!' He was quite brazen when Madame Berthe remonstrated with him. 'I've got a great technique and I intend to show it off.'

It was the arrival of the newspapers in the early hours of the morning that changed his tune. Such was the esteem in which James George was held, that although the ballet had been presented by a small, provincial company, most of the London dailies had sent critics to the première. Not one of them seemed to have enjoyed the experience.

As Vronsky, David Bryant showed that he has yet to learn that if overall excellence is to be maintained, the whole is greater than the parts. He performed with skill and virtuosity, but with no sense of balance or proportion. Perhaps a more experienced ballerina could have kept his worst excesses in check, but as Anna, Georgina George was too young and immature to do so.

They had all said much the same — that by his determination to dazzle, David had upset the delicate balance of the ballet, and that his ballerina had not managed to prevent it.

Gina knew they were right. She had watched David dance the part with

Alicia Allen, had witnessed how the older woman could bring out a passion in his performance while keeping a firm rein on his desire to show off.

'They don't know what they're talking about!' David shouted, flinging the papers on the floor. 'The British have never appreciated home-grown talent — just wait till I'm in the States!'

Gina hoped the proposed American tour by the Eastern, to which she supposed he must be referring, did come off. He would be even angrier if it didn't. He turned and stormed towards the exit, and she ran swiftly after him.

'What do you want?' He glowered at her.

'Let me come with you,' she begged, hating to feel shut out of any part of his life, even in his failure. He gave a curt nod.

David drove in silence to his flat, but once inside he had another outburst.

'Those damned critics can't see talent when it's staring them in the face! Saying I spoiled the ballet . . . I'd like to see them try to work up a passion for a schoolgirl like you!'

Gina blinked in hurt surprise, but he gave her no time to make a reply.

'Couldn't they see I had to dance like that to give the ballet any interest at all? Your performance was hardly going to enthral them, and as for your emotional development . . . ' He gave an unpleasant laugh.

He raged on, blaming her for the failure of the ballet and accusing her of ruining his career. Young though she was, she thought she understood: he was like a hurt child hitting out at the one nearest to him to try and ease his pain, and she only wished she could help him.

'David,' her soft voice interrupted him, 'I know you are disappointed, we both are, but we have the rest of our lives together. Let's get married as soon as possible — '

'You must be joking!' His spiteful laugh resounded round the room. 'You believe getting married will make it up to me? Do you really suppose I'd fancy a prissy innocent like you? I only proposed because you were James George's daughter! Why do you think I have never pushed for more than a peck on the cheek from you? You're the most passionless woman I have ever met, as cold as ice!'

That was when he really started to berate her, deprecating her attractions as a woman. Mercifully the ringing of the doorbell had broken off his flood of invective, and Gina stood immobile in the corner as he went to answer it.

'Hello, lover-boy,' a female voice, husky and mid-western, reached her ears. 'I came to commiserate.'

The tall blonde Gina had first seen in David's dressing-room at the Coliseum entered carrying a bottle of champagne. She saw the younger girl's trembling body and went over to her.

'What's the matter, honey? He been giving you a bad time?'

Gina was so shocked she was unable to speak.

'Look, he's not worth worrying about.' The older girl was not unkind. 'You're too sweet and young for him.'

'God knows I never wanted her!' David spat out. 'I only became involved with her to get her father's attention! I wanted the chance to get ahead more quickly than I was with the National, and as the contract you offered me didn't start until next month, I decided to come here.'

'Contract, what contract?' Gina's teeth were chattering, and she only just managed the question. The blonde put her arm around her.

'A five-year contract as principal soloist with the Iowa State Ballet,' she explained.

'But — but you can't go! What about the Eastern? With Anthony May leaving we won't have anyone — '

'Tough!'

It was the last word David ever said to her, for the American woman insisted on driving her home. Her father met her at the door, and she sobbed on his shoulder her apologies for the failure of the ballet.

'That's all right, Swan Princess, I should never have let you dance Anna.'

Proof positive that it had been her fault. She trusted her father's judgment absolutely. He had only accepted David as May's successor at her instigation — and look how it had turned out.

But worse than that had been believing David's accusation of her frozen emotions . . .

* * *

Now that aching hurt was gone. She had learned her reactions were as open and responsive as anyone else's — indeed, perhaps even more so following the long, cold winter in her heart. No longer did she feel bowed down by remorse and sadness — her feelings were as buoyant and fresh as the sixteen-year-old Princess Aurora whom she was to dance that night. And he was going to watch her.

'It's my favourite ballet,' Jude had

said when he found out, proving yet again that he was more knowledgeable about dancing than she had initially suspected, and she determined to give her all to this, her first *Sleeping Beauty* of the season.

After all, she owed him a lot — he had broken the legacy of fear and loathing for herself that David's cruel words had left, and gradually he was teaching her to trust again.

And perhaps by shining in Beauty I can make amends for Karenina, she thought, for she knew the old classic was more suited to her style than was the more modern work.

She was glad Jude had not seen her as Anna. She knew he thought her a promising dancer — the more so since she had let up on administration and paid more attention to class — and would have hated to think he had witnessed such abject failure. For she was finding she wanted him to see her only at her best, and wondered why it should matter so much to her.

'Lover boy coming back today?' Amelia's giggles interrupted Gina's reverie, and she gritted her teeth to reply.

'Jude Alexander returns from France this morning, if that's what you mean.'

She had tried to play down their friendship, not keen to have others know her business, but the younger girl was an incurable romantic and had refused to accept the assurance that they were just good friends.

'Lucky you. He's what I call a real man, not like the wimps I seem to attract.' Amelia grinned. 'He could put his slippers under my bed any time!'

'I'll tell him.' Gina's voice was tight. 'He certainly won't get the opportunity with me.'

Now why did I say that? she wondered as Amelia walked away laughing. *Is it because secretly that's just what I want him to do, and am too afraid to admit it?*

It was hard to tell. She had spent little time with Jude after the gala and none of that alone, for he had departed on a two-week business trip only days later. He had called at the Little Theatre to say goodbye, where he had kissed her chastely on the lips in full view of the talkative Amelia.

'We'll continue this — um — conversation when I get back,' he had murmured, his throbbing voice sending delicious shivers down to her toes, and she had nodded her acquiescence.

She had received a couple of cryptically worded postcards from him, both of which she had read many times over and now carried around with her in her handbag, and she found herself counting the days till his return with feverish impatience.

But she didn't immediately realise how often her thoughts turned to him: to his dark, probing eyes, his muscular frame and towering height; to the way his hair fell over his forehead; to his voice, his power, the urgency of his kiss . . . Her heart lurched alarmingly as she suddenly accepted he had become her obsession.

It was understandable when the facts were considered. She had come to him verbally bruised and abused, and once he had freed her from David's curse, she had turned to him in gratitude. He was a very exciting man, his potent masculinity had seared her with its heat and intensity, and she was ripe for the taking.

Never before had she felt the way she did when he touched her, never experienced the aching need his nearness caused in her and like all new experiences, it took some getting used to. It was heady and earth-shattering, yes, but there was also a darker side . . . one of fear and doubt.

She tried not to think of that, but occasionally she would worry — was Jude sincere, could she trust him to keep his word? Only time would tell, but she knew how desperately hurt she would be if he did not.

She realised now that her subconscious had diagnosed the attraction from their first meeting, but believing herself unacceptably cold, she had tried to explain away the tell-tale signs. The dangerous desires she had put down as reminders of her affair with David, her fearful longings to worry about what Jude could do to the Eastern. She had tried to kid herself because she didn't want him to get the upper hand, to gain a lever to use against her, but finally, she had stopped fooling herself. She had not dared to admit even inwardly how badly she had wanted the man himself.

'That will be all, ladies and gentlemen.' Madame Berthe's muted voice brought her back to reality, and she saw the ballet mistress beckon her over.

'Yes, Madame?'

'I am very pleased with your progress, Gina.' The older woman smiled. 'Now go and enjoy yourself this afternoon. Try to put *Beauty* out of your mind and relax.'

Gina nodded, and wandered back to the flat to get changed. She doubted she would see Jude before the evening performance — he would have a lot of work to catch up on as this was his first day back in England — so she decided to sit in the garden.

The weather was marvellous for the time of year, and she found herself almost guiltily grateful for the greenhouse effect. She padded out to the bottom of the garden in shorts and flip-flops, and flung herself down on an old tartan rug — in the shade, to ensure she obeyed Madame Berthe's sunbathing embargo on the dancers.

She stretched languidly in the warmth. Birds sang overhead and a gentle breeze worried the long grass around her, the soft rustling vying pleasantly with the quiet hum of distant traffic. She closed her eyes and dreamed of Jude, taking her mind back over their every meeting: Jude in his immaculate Italian suit, even the expensive tailoring unable to disguise completely his muscular, male frame; Jude in full evening dress, turning heads at the dinner-dance; Jude as countryman in cords and boots, his animal magnetism smouldering just beneath the surface. And she remembered too, the way his eyes creased with laughter when he was amused, fine lines radiating good humour; the way his dark hair just covered his ears and curled in the nape of his neck; the determined set of his jaw and the sensual line of his mouth. She drifted in and out of sleep, remembering the expert way he had awakened her frozen emotions. Her eyelids grew heavy, and she dreamed he was by her side, holding her tightly.

In her dream, she returned his embrace, and curled her fingers in his dark hair. He felt so warm and so alive, and she thrilled to his touch.

'Darling girl!' he whispered in her ear, and she awoke with a jolt, but found she didn't want to withdraw from his embrace. 'I've missed you so much. Madame Berthe told me she had seen you come into the garden, so I came looking for you, and when I saw you lying here, so beautiful, I couldn't stop myself.' He pressed his mouth down on hers, and finally she understood what people meant when they said the earth moved.

'I don't think I want you to stop,' she murmured huskily, when he eventually broke free. 'I can't believe this is happening to me. I used to think I was a cold person.'

Jude gave a hoot of derisive laughter, which increased to a deep, throaty chuckle, warm and appreciative, and she had to admit it did not sound unkind.

'What on earth gave you that idea — or should I say who?'

She looked away, unable to meet his gaze.

'Dear David again.' He knew at once. 'You little fool — didn't you realise that by accusing you he was only covering up for his own inadequacies?'

'You don't understand, I felt nothing with him — not like I do with you. It was my fault — '

He caught her wrists. 'Your fault?' he asked huskily, and once again his mouth sought hers.

A burning ache rose inside her, blood singing in her ears at his onslaught, and she wound her arms around his neck, fingers raking his sleek, dark hair.

'Your fault?' he murmured again. 'Surely I've just put the lie to that? Face it, Gina, David couldn't turn you on, and it was that inability coupled with his refusal to accept the fact, that made him castigate you.'

She drew a little apart from him, hypnotised by his stare. Her breathing was erratic and her hands trembled as she considered what he had said. Could it be true — that the missing spark had been more David's fault than hers?

It would explain a lot, especially his fury when she had offered him a gift he could not handle — to marry her at once. Was it really as simple as that — David had been unable to awaken her?

'I suppose you could be right,' she said at last.

'Good girl!' He stroked her hair out of her face. 'I really believe you are over

David. Do you fancy having a meal with me at Melrose House after your performance tonight?'

Her heart sang as she acknowledged that oh, how she wanted to be with him.

Later, when she was dancing on stage, she realised how much she owed Jude. He had shown her that she needed to allow her emotional life to grow, and having done so, she found her interpretation had a depth it had never attained before.

She had always enjoyed *Sleeping Beauty* with its three sharply contrasting acts which meant the ballerina was able to demonstrate three different facets in performance: the radiant youthfulness and gaiety of Act One; the exquisite, disembodied spirit of the vision scene; and finally the mature woman at her wedding.

Previously, Gina realised her Aurora had been much the same in both Acts One and Three — joyful, bouncy and spontaneous — with a contrast offered only in Act Two, where she became the

192

floaty, enchanted princess. Tonight however, it was different; Gina knew that her Aurora in Act Three had developed into a rounder, more complete person from the child in Act One.

An awakening indeed, she thought, seeing the character in a completely new light. The kiss did not just herald the opening of Aurora's eyes and the ending of a great sleep, but also the opening of her heart and emotions to the arrival of a lover, a dawning of romance.

As she acknowledged the applause at the end of her solo, she knew she was also acknowledging something far more basic — that she herself had been awakened by Jude's loving. He had taken her from her self-imposed emotional prison, and set her free. She did not kid herself he would be an easy man to love . . . but she knew she wanted to try.

'That was excellent, Gina!' Alicia Allen was waiting for her when, she came offstage. She was wearing a heavy shawl wrapped around her to combat the wicked draughts that all theatres seemed to have, even in the height of summer.

Gina flushed with pride. For the prima ballerina to congratulate her was praise indeed, especially as Alicia must have come into the wings expressly to watch her.

She looked about her and realised there was an unusually large number of people standing around, old dressing gowns or towels draped over tights and underclothes as a sop to decency, and all eyes seemed to be on her. As a professional she knew the compliment her fellow dancers were paying her — word must have buzzed around backstage that her dancing tonight was something special, and as quickly as the jungle telegraph travelled, they had trooped to the sides of the stage to watch her performance.

'You're maturing into a wonderful Beauty.' Alicia smiled. 'I can see I'll be leaving the company in safe hands.'

Gina could only manage a stumbling word of thanks, too over-awed to say more, but inwardly she glowed. Years of hard, unceasing work with many ballet mistresses had gone into making her fairy-tale princess; it had taken one man only a single afternoon to teach her how to be a woman.

She took her bouquets and padded in her ballet slippers back to her dressing-room. Jude was waiting for her there, chatting easily to her father, and just for a moment a sharp chill passed through her heart as she wondered what they were talking about. Did it still concern a partnership, she worried — and had this afternoon been a calculated move for Jude towards attaining that goal?

'Princess, you were amazing!' James George enthused. 'You've never done a better Beauty.'

'You were magnificent,' Jude agreed, and kissed her lightly on the cheek. 'I was just telling James about our dinner date — advising him not to wait up for you.'

'Why not let her stay overnight?' James said. 'It'll be a heck of a trek for you to bring Gina home and then return to Melrose.'

'That's a great idea.' Jude nodded his approval. 'What do you say, Gina?'

'Fine by me.' But Gina was surprised by her father's attitude. Not because he was happy for her to stay at Melrose House — her parents had always kept her on a very loose rein — but because he so clearly liked and admired Jude Alexander. She had not had enough boyfriends to know if James would run true to the stereotypical jealous father — although he had never said so, she had sensed he had not liked David. Now it looked as if he was only too pleased to entrust her to Jude.

She wondered again why her father had accepted David as Anthony May's successor. She appreciated now that he had not wanted to — had not thought the boy good enough — yet he had given in to Gina's pleas.

Today even Gina comprehended that

while her fiancé had been good, he lacked the discipline to be outstanding, and quality was the god at whose door James worshipped, so why? It was a puzzle.

'How long will it take you to change?'

She gave a start as she realised Jude was talking to her, and pulled her thoughts back to the present.

'About half an hour,' she assessed. 'OK?'

He nodded and departed with her father, and again Gina felt that stab of fear as she noticed how deep they were in conversation.

This is crazy, she thought, *I'll go mad if I suspect Jude every time I see him with Dad*. Was it just David's treatment that left her so suspicious of being used, or was it something more fundamental — the fact that whereas she had been fond of her fiancé, her feelings for Jude were altogether more complex and demanding?

She dressed carefully after her shower, wanting to look as sophisticated and elegant as the women she was sure Jude usually escorted, but nervous over her choice of clothes. She had decided finally to lay the ghost and wear the black outfit she had bought for the première of *Karenina*.

'Very nice,' was all Jude said as she shimmied towards him, but the way he was regarding her said a great deal more.

They drove in companionable silence to Melrose House.

'This way.' He opened the front door. 'I asked Mrs Hicks, my housekeeper, to leave us a cold compilation in the drawing room.'

It proved to be a feast. They started with individual quiches — dainty little cases which melted on the tongue, the crisp, golden pastry crumbling lightly at the touch. Then came a cold plate of asparagus, baby peas, tiny new potatoes and trout en gelée with a thick, rich mayonnaise. She had the dancer's usual hearty appetite, and he was amused to watch her tuck in.

She saw that she had an audience.

'You'll have to get used to hungry dancers if you're going to get involved with the Eastern. We're all trencher-men, you know.' She spoke without thinking, and could have bitten off her tongue when she saw his hopeful expression. She had not meant to encourage his offer, but the words had just slipped out, and she had to admit the idea of Jude being around for most of the day had suddenly taken on a definite appeal.

Yet she didn't want things to move too fast. She needed time to make sure the right decision was being made — that she was not, once again, making a fool of herself over a man who didn't want her — merely her father's company.

'Your dancing was fantastic tonight.' Jude handed her a glass of wine. 'Pathos, poetry, drama — you had all three. Per-fection!' and he raised his glass to toast her before taking a sip.

'Thank you. I felt different, I know.

When Prince Florimund kissed me from sleep I suddenly understood the allegory of the awakening — that Aurora was experiencing real love for the first time — and I realised I was portraying her truthfully for the first time in my life, too.'

'Because you had experienced the same emotions yourself recently?' He was watching her intently and his voice held an urgency she could not understand, as if there were something he particularly wanted to hear her say.

'Well, I suppose it must have had some bearing on it' — she was loath to admit how much — 'though, of course, we are not in love.' She wanted to make it clear she understood the rules of the game: neither of them was looking for love, and she was determined he should realise she did not intend to fall praising at his feet.

Later, snuggled into the tester bed in the guest bedroom, some lines from a poem came to her:

He either fears his fate too much,

Or his deserts are small,
That dares not put it to the touch,
To gain or lose it all.
Well, she would dare.

8

Over the next few weeks Gina felt happier than she had been since her mother had died, and she was honest enough to admit that a great part of that was down to Jude.

Since her stay at Melrose Hall he had taken her out on a number of occasions, and the more she got to know him, the better she liked him. She had seen him quite often and as she learned more about him, she came to realise that the role she had originally cast him in — that of a heartless, money-driven Philistine — wasn't the truth at all. He might be a successful businessman, and she was sure he drove a hard bargain, but he could also be fun; she couldn't remember laughing so much for a long time.

'It's good to see you enjoying yourself again, Princess.'

Gina noticed her father had lost the haunted look he'd acquired after his wife's death, as if a great weight had been lifted off his chest, and, she realised, she felt the same way, too. Mr Lindt giving them the breathing space to regroup had certainly made a difference, and meant she no longer spent so much time on the dreaded paperwork.

She supposed she'd have to get back to it eventually, but for the moment she just wanted to dance and to enjoy herself. She was working exceptionally hard in class, and although she had always striven for perfection, she knew that today she had a new goal: she wanted to impress Jude. She recognised now that he was an informed balletomane, and more than that, that his approval was very important to her. For he had taught her to believe in herself and to trust again.

'Why would you let a spoilt, self-indulgent egoist define you?' he had asked her once, and it had given her pause for thought. Why would she?

She came to accept that hero-worship mixed up with adolescence had blunted her critical faculties, meaning it wasn't so much foolish as understandable that she had fallen for David.

She had been mesmerised by his glamour — the rising star in an international company who mixed with such sophisticates in his dressing-room. And she had been at the age when girls fell in love with the idea of being in love, and who better to fall for than the confident, older dancer?

But had she really ever loved him? Once she had thought so, but the feelings she was experiencing with Jude — and when she was alone and thought about him — were so different, and so much more real and exciting, that now she doubted it.

She pulled herself up sharply. She was being ridiculous! She wasn't in love with Jude, she couldn't be; she simply enjoyed his company.

Whatever she felt for him, she should never forget that his first interest had been in the Eastern, not in her. He might have proved to be a pleasant — even special — companion, but her first interest should be the Eastern, too, to ensure it retained its independence.

Still, she was enjoying life in the moment. No looking back at past failures, no looking forward to pessimistic futures; today was enough.

Then came the phone call. She had been at a costume fitting in Boundary Road when she answered the shrilling phone to the news that would change her life.

'Gina? Thank goodness I've got you.' Jude's voice was urgent. 'Now, listen, get straight to Branchester General Hospital.'

She tensed. 'Why?'

'It's your father — '

She drew in her breath and he hurried on.

'Look, try not to worry, it'll be OK — '

'But what's happened!' she demanded. 'Tell me, tell me!'

'I think James has had a stroke — '

'When . . . how?' again she interrupted, a cold terror creeping through
her. *Daddy, Daddy*, she wanted to cry,
oh, please don't leave me!

'A quarter of an hour ago. Luckily, I
was with him, so I dialled nine-nine-
nine at once . . . Oh, here's the
ambulance — I've got to go. I'll see you
at the hospital.'

'All right . . . oh, and Jude, tell Dad I
love him.'

* * *

The journey to the hospital was one of
the worst of Gina's life. She sat on the
edge of the seat and rocked forwards as
if by so doing she could urge the taxi
faster on its way. Her mind flooded
with images of her father: James the
choreographer taking rehearsals, the
inevitable cigarette in hand; James the
father, reading her bedtime stories with
such conviction that she had trembled
under the bedclothes all night when he
had introduced her to the wicked witch

in *Snow White*; James the husband, arm casually draped over Marjory's shoulders, protective eyes only for her.

She could not bear it. She had always loved her parents so dearly that losing her mother had been a dreadful blow; her life would be empty without James too.

Well, not completely empty, perhaps — Jude had begun to teach her about another kind of loving. Thank goodness she had Jude to support her through this difficult time . . .

But did she have him? Now that push came to shove, she wasn't sure. Why had he been with her father? He had promised not to press on with his goal to buy into the Eastern unless he was invited. Had he been trying to persuade James in spite of his promise? And what if the stress of it had caused a stroke? She forced her hands into small, tight fists, biting her lip to control the virulent thoughts that assailed her.

What an idiot she was to have believed Jude — his promise to leave the Eastern alone had obviously been so much hot air, and once he thought he had won her round — got her to lower her defences — he must have hot-footed it round to her father to try and attain his dream. She remembered all his sweet endearments, and mocked herself for being so naïve as to think he meant them. As if an experienced sophisticate like Jude Alexander would really be interested in her!

Hot tears filled her eyes, and she hung her head lest the taxi driver should see them. *Pull yourself together*, she chastised herself, *you're not the first woman to be used by a man — even if you were stupid enough to let history repeat itself.*

However, telling herself the fact did not make it any easier to bear. But what had she expected — that a businessman's word was his bond? Not when money was involved, surely?

And yet . . . as far as she knew, no money was involved in Jude's convoluted project, so was it just a dislike of being crossed that had made him so determined to control the Eastern? Had he become as obsessed with his dream as she was with hers? For she did not kid herself that learning the truth about the man had in any way lessened the way her body reacted to him. Even though she now suspected him of being both a liar and a cheat, still she burned with the memory of his closeness, and her lips puckered unconsciously at the thought of his kisses.

The car stopped outside the entrance to the Accident and Emergency Department, and Gina rushed in. Jude was waiting for her by the door, and when she saw him her treacherous heart lurched, and she had to grip her hands together fiercely when he kissed her to prevent herself returning his embrace.

'It's OK, Gina.' Jude put his arm around her to steady her. 'The doctors are with your father at the moment. It looks like we got here in time.'

No thanks to you! she thought, and then frowned. What was it about the

Eastern that was so important to him that he was prepared to hound her father for it? She supposed there was some tax advantage in taking over a failing company, but doubted the gain was large enough to mean much to Relly Holdings.

Perhaps it was the idea of being a patron of the Arts that attracted Jude — after all, having spent thousands on his theatre, he obviously didn't mean to do things by halves. But still she couldn't rid herself of the feeling that there was more to it than met the eye — that there was some secret reason why Jude wanted the Eastern which he was not prepared to discuss.

'Miss George?' A nurse appeared from behind the screened-off cubicle. 'You can see your father now.'

Jude made to accompany her, but Gina dismissed him with icy disdain.

'No, I'll go alone.'

He looked surprised, but did not argue, and she stepped inside, afraid of what she might see. James was lying on a high trolley, a blue blanket covering him. His face was grey and strained, and he looked small and frail under the bright lights and frighteningly hi-tech equipment. A nurse bustled efficiently around the prone figure taking observations and charting them on a clipboard on the bed-table, while two white-coated doctors were studying the print-out from an ominous looking machine, discussing the results quietly.

'Oh, Dad!' Gina rushed to his side and clasped the left hand that he awkwardly proffered.

He gave her a lop-sided grin and tried to say hello, but it came out as a strangled cry, and her heart went out to him as he struggled to make himself understood.

'Darling, don't worry.' She bent forward and kissed him. 'I know it's frightening for you at the moment, but you'll get better soon. And you're not to worry about the company . . .'

James gave a slight nod, and with his good hand, began to rummage among his possessions on the locker beside him. Finally he located what he was searching for and passed it over to her.

It was a business card for Jude Alexander.

She understood, and thought how ironic it was that her father was recommending she lean on the very man whose single-minded pursuit had undoubtedly added to the stress which had caused his stroke! And by capitulating, she had given Jude carte blanche to pester James. He had tricked her into thinking he really cared about her, and she hated herself for being so gullible. She should have been more cautious, but looking back on it, she saw how cleverly Jude had gone about getting his own way, playing her like a finely tuned violin since the moment they had met.

Guilt, more guilt — would it never end?

'We're sending your father to the ward,' the nurse explained. 'Why don't you go home? He'll be asleep soon, and you can't do anything here.'

Gina threw her father an agonised

glance, and he managed a twisted smile and gave her a thumbs-up. The house-man followed her out.

'How is he?' she asked, and Jude came to join her.

'Well, as I told Mr Alexander, your father has had a minor stroke. With a bit of luck his condition will stabilise, and then we'll start intensive rehabilitation, to try and regain as much use of his body as possible.'

Gina nodded her understanding. A thousand questions flooded her mind. *Would he ever dance again?* she wanted to ask. *Could he deteriorate — oh, God, might he even die?* But she did not dare in case the answers were more than she could bear.

Jude took her by the elbow and guided her to the exit, where she shrugged off his arm and turned to face him.

'Why did the doctors report on James' condition to you? I'm his daughter. You aren't even a relative.'

He spoke as if soothing a fractious child.

213

'If you had been here, they would have talked to you. They told me because I was the person with him when he came in.'

'Of course you were with him,' she spluttered, 'and if it wasn't for you harrying him, he wouldn't have had a stroke!'

'What are you talking about?' One black brow raised with the question, and for a moment Gina was afraid, but there was no turning back.

'You know very well! Oh, you were clever — I grant you that — convincing me you were fond of me so that I'd drop my guard. But your word doesn't count for much, does it? The moment I trusted you, you rushed round to Boundary Road to try and get James to agree to your demands.'

'Really?' He was deceptively calm. 'And when did you make this momentous discovery?'

'I realised what an idiot I'd been to believe you in the taxi on the way here. That I can live with, it's the knowledge that my stupidity let you hound my father until he had a stroke that really gets me down. Not that such niceties would worry you, would they? Just so long as you get your way.'

'How astute of you to realise James is not my main concern.'

His voice was level, but she saw the angry pulse at his temple. So he was admitting his guilt.

'You cold-hearted beast!' she cried, and tried to back away from him, but he caught her and pulled her closer to him.

'You didn't seem to find me so cold-blooded when we kissed last night,' he said, white with rage.

She glared at him. 'I hate you!' It came out as a sob, and she kicked him on the shins to get away. The pain forced him to let go, and she heard him curse as she made her escape down the long ramp that lead to the street.

She hurried towards Boundary Road, a strange weariness descending over her. She didn't understand how life could continue as normal, when inside she was dying. Somehow it seemed quite wrong that as her father lay desperately ill, things should carry on regardless. Jude Alexander — how she hated the man! But even as his name sprang to mind, her traitorous body betrayed her, and a spasm of longing stopped her in her tracks.

'No,' she gasped, 'surely not?'

But there could be no denial. Amoral, untrustworthy, dishonest as he was, still he held a mesmeric attraction for her. However much she wanted to be rid of him, his powerful magnetism would always win — and the knowledge of that truth filled her with self-loathing at her own weakness.

How could she want the man whose actions had resulted in such a catastrophic outcome for her father? It was as if he had taken over her own will.

★ ★ ★

'Gina, how is James?'

News of her father's illness had

filtered through to the company, and when she entered the Garden Studio, the dancers had collected together in small groups, all urgently discussing the situation. Their voices were muted and their smiles in her direction sympathetic, but she felt a certain tension in the air.

'Are we going to be able to carry on without your father — until he gets better, I mean?'

She didn't blame the dancers for their questions: without James they were worried their jobs might be on the line, and there was nothing she could say to reassure them. At the moment she was as much in the dark as they were — having not the slightest idea whether or not the company could withstand its founder's enforced absence.

'I hope so,' she said. When her mother had died, Gina had been able to step into the breach. This time there was no one available.

She did not kid herself that she could stand in for her father as well — apart from the fact that as a choreographer he was unique, she knew she had not made such a fantastic job of the administration, especially since Mr Lindt's second loan — and she had the humility to accept she could do no more.

Madame Berthe read the despair in her star pupil's body language, and clapped her hands together. 'Come along, come along. Of course we are all worried about James, but he would be the first to insist we must go on as normal. So take your places at the barre, please.'

Gina tried hard to concentrate on class, but had some terrifying lapses of memory. What were they going to do? She knew she would have to relieve her father from all worry so she could not discuss the company with him, but she needed someone to bounce ideas against.

Also, she was concerned about what would happen when the bank found out that James was incapacitated. She had a horrible suspicion that Mr Lindt might decide this was the straw to break the camel's back and call in their loan.

'My dear,' Madame Berthe caught Gina's hands at the end of the lesson as the other dancers filed out, 'try not to despair. Your father is a fighter — he has always had an indomitable spirit — I'm sure he'll be all right. Don't worry.'

'Oh, Madame, I hope you're right! But it's not just Dad I worry about — I'm terrified that when news of his illness gets out, people will lose confidence in our ability to continue and stay away from the theatre. I just don't know where to turn for advice.'

'What about Jude Alexander?' The irony of her suggestion was lost on Madame Berthe. 'I'm sure he'd help you. Have you thought of asking him?'

'Ask Jude Alexander?' Gina could not believe what she was hearing. 'Madame, don't you see? It's because of him that Dad's where he is.'

'I heard he took your father to hospital — '

'I don't mean that,' she broke in impatiently. 'Jude Alexander caused James's stroke. He badgered and badgered him about becoming a partner, and finally the stress proved too much.'

'I don't think — '

'Well I *know!*' Gina refused to listen to any excuses for the man. As far as she was concerned, he had no redeeming features. 'He hasn't stopped making a nuisance of himself since he first became interested in the Eastern. Don't you remember when Mr Lindt brought him backstage at the Little? He admitted they'd been talking business with Dad that afternoon, and I'm pretty sure he told James I was skipping classes to deal with the administration, too. All he had to do was feed Dad the idea it was his fault my dancing was suffering because he was working me too hard, and James would have felt horribly guilty. Stress like that has brought on this stroke.'

Madame Berthe looked as if she was about to say something, but seeing the glint in Gina's eye she thought better of it and merely gave her a doubtful glance.

As she departed, Gina sighed. It was clear the ballet mistress thought she was being uncharitable — but then Madame Berthe did not know the full story, and Gina certainly did not intend to tell her.

Wearily she made towards the door. She knew she ought to be in the office — she had been very lax since Mr Lindt had eased up on their loan and had let things pile up — but wished she could put off the evil hour. Hell must be an office, she decided, with masses of back paperwork to clear.

An hour later she was heading for the manager's office at the Little Theatre. It was larger than the one at Boundary Road, and in even more of a muddle.

She walked in, and was startled to see someone, back to the door, rifling through the papers on the desk. Then she recognised the lionesque head of Jude Alexander.

'What on earth do you think you are doing here?' Her mouth felt dry. 'How dare you rummage through our private papers?'

'I'm not rummaging, and they're not private, at least, not from me.' His voice was impersonal. 'And what I'm trying to do is make some sense out of the mess you've left here on this desk.'

'Get out!' She didn't trust herself to say more. 'Just get out of here!'

He made no move to leave.

'I haven't finished yet.'

She gritted her teeth. 'I'll — I'll call the police!' she threatened, but he merely smiled.

'And tell them what? That you suspect me of being a thief? You forget, there's nothing here worth stealing.'

Her mind was racing. Was he so sure of the outcome of her father's illness that he felt there was no need to hide his intentions any longer? she wondered. After all, as a businessman he had the ear of the financial community, and even if James recovered quickly, it would not be difficult for Jude to spread alarm among their creditors.

'You hateful man!' she cried. 'You never meant to keep your word at all, did you? All that rubbish about not taking over unless I asked you — '

'I didn't say unless *you* asked me. If you remember, the deal was I would only come on board if I was invited, and I have been . . . by James.'

Her mouth opened and shut involuntarily as she understood she had been tricked.

'When — when did he ask you?' she demanded.

'This morning, before he had his stroke.'

'Before you caused his stroke, you mean! And you would say that, wouldn't you, now that he's unable to talk for himself? But I shall ask him later, you just see if I don't! He's still able to nod his head — '

'No!' His voice rapped out like a gun shot. 'You will not trouble James!'

'Frightened he'll put the lie to your claim?' she taunted, and then realised she had gone too far as he crossed the room, the pared lines of his face set hard against her.

'I am not frightened of that, no, but I refuse to let you jeopardise his safe recovery by troubling him with your childish pique!'

'Childish pique!' she echoed furiously.

'Yes, you obviously misunderstood what I meant when we struck our bargain, and now you don't like the thought of me getting the upper hand.'

'You haven't got the upper hand yet — '

'No? So you really are selfish enough to upset your father in his present state with worries about the Eastern?'

Gina faltered, knowing that she was not. She was stymied, beaten by a master of the art of double-speak, and she resented the fact vehemently.

'All right,' she capitulated, 'you win for now. But I won't forget this!'

He was unimpressed.

'Then your memory must have improved since you received these letters.' He waved a hand at the papers in front of him. 'Tell me, don't you ever reply to correspondence?'

'I haven't had time — '

'My point exactly, you were trying to do too much. I rest my case.' The phone rang and he sat on the side of the desk to answer it. 'Hello? Yes . . . could you hold the line one moment, please?' He put his hand over the mouthpiece and nodded at her. 'Don't let me keep you. You're expected on stage for rehearsal.'

She glared at him. How dared he dismiss her from her own office in that arrogant fashion? She wished she could think of a suitably cutting reply, but the shock of finding him there seemed to have frozen her wits, and she had to content herself with slamming the door loudly as she left.

Had her father really asked Jude to join them, she wondered, or had the predatory businessman made the whole thing up?

It was hard to tell, but if Jude had managed to convince James he was overworking Gina, it was just possible, especially if he had hinted that in spite of all her efforts the books were not in good order. Another thought struck her — her father was not oblivious of the relationship that had been developing between Jude and herself, and it could be, that in view of her softening attitude, he had thought she would like Jude close at hand. After all, was that not the reason he had employed David — because he knew it would please her?

'I hear Jude Alexander is to be administrator.' Madame Berthe joined her in the foyer, a question mark in her voice. 'His business experience should be of great help to you.'

How news travels, thought Gina crossly, but, 'Yes, I expect so,' was all she said. She refused to divulge her feelings on the matter, but secretly admitted that what the ballet mistress said was true. The office work cried out for a more organised brain than hers, and the knowledge that she would not have to shut herself away with the ledgers again was a tremendous relief. In fact, if her liberator had been anyone other than Jude Alexander, she would have been delighted by her release.

Later that day, Jude called a meeting of all the company to introduce himself. Listening to his speech, Gina could tell he was making a good impression, and saw her fellow performers relax as they felt more secure in their jobs.

'Things are not going to be easy,' he said. 'The company's finances are shaky and the future looks uncertain.'

She clenched her jaw, taking what he said as a personal attack on her handling of the situation up until then, even though she knew he was only stating a fact.

'I believe in the Eastern,' he continued, 'and I hope you do, too. I know if we all pull together, we can get out of the red, and put the company back on a sound footing.'

An excited buzz broke out among the dancers, but Gina noted with satisfaction that the stagehands had not been won over — though she was surprised to see that Stan wasn't present. But Jude had news there, too.

'I also have to tell you that Stan has resigned. We had a private talk and he decided it was time to move on.'

'Good job!' the wardrobe mistress broke in. 'I for one certainly didn't give him the right to talk for me, but he could be very intimidating.'

'Well he won't be intimidating anyone here any more. I understand that he told you the dancers had had pay rises and you felt aggrieved because you hadn't, which was why he threatened strike action. I'm here to tell you that he was misinformed — no one in the company has had a pay rise for two years. I admit that's a pretty dreadful state of affairs, but unless we all pull together now, no one ever will.'

A hum of indignant chatter broke out among the backstage crew.

'But he said everyone else had had a huge pay increase,' one addressed Jude.

'Well, he lied,' Jude said, and he

turned on his heel and left.

Even Gina was impressed. For months Stan's complaints had caused her a great deal of inconvenience, and she had never bested him. But it seemed Jude had managed to get to the bottom of his complaints and prove them baseless, leading to the trouble-maker's resignation. She hated to admit it, but perhaps her father had been right to invite a businessman to help . . . if James had in fact done so, of course.

She looked at her watch. There was just time to visit him before the evening performance, so she changed swiftly and ran down to the bus stop. The familiar red Porsche drew up beside her.

'Going to see James? Hop in. I'm going there myself.'

'Thank you, I prefer to wait for the bus.'

'Don't be stupid, Gina. What's the point of waiting here when you could spend that time with your father? Besides, we ought to show him a united

229

front.' He climbed out of the car and joined her on the pavement. 'Come on.' He held open the passenger door, and as they were gathering an interested audience from the bus queue, she felt obliged to get in.

'James will be glad to see us together,' Jude said as they drove off.

'What do you mean?' Her voice was cold.

'Well, you've hardly made it a secret that you don't want me to become part of the Eastern, so he was rather worried about how you'd react when he asked me to do so. If we appear to be good terms when we visit him, he'll be reassured that you approve of his decision.'

She gave him a glacial look.

'I don't approve of it. I'm not even sure I believe you when you say he asked you to join us.'

'No?' He seemed amused by her obstinacy. 'Too bad,' and his voice took on a warning tone. 'You don't want to upset your father, do you? He's got a pretty good idea of how near bankruptcy the company is, and if he thought you had to cope with that on your own, he would be very worried indeed.'

She glared at him. 'And who told him we're almost bankrupt, I should like to know? James wouldn't be aware of our finances unless someone like you had pointed it out to him!'

'You're wrong,' he countered. 'I've told you before, you underestimate your father. He's not some absent-minded professor, you know, he's quite able to read a balance sheet.'

'You and I seem to know two different James Georges.'

'Yes, we do indeed. The question is, are you prepared to risk your James having a relapse to prove a point?'

'What do you mean?' She was very suspicious.

'Just this. You tell your father you refuse to work with me, and the worry could hinder his recovery. Is that what you want?'

She wished she could tell him to go to hell, but what if he was telling the truth about her father's invitation? And if she believed stress was the cause of James' stroke, how could she add to his problems? Jude had out-manoeuvred her once again, and the look he gave her told her he knew he had.

'OK,' she capitulated, 'you win this time — I'll pretend we are the best of buddies in front of Dad. But don't expect it to last. The moment he's better, I'll tell him the truth and you'll have to leave.'

The car screeched to a stop as he pulled over to the side of the road.

'Now, you listen to me — ' his face was inches from her own — 'whether you like it or not, we're going to work together! The experience can be as good or as bad as you choose to make it, but I don't expect any back-stabbing or behind-the-scenes intrigue — do I make myself clear?'

Her sharp intake of breath indicated her anger, but she only gave a tense nod, aware this was not the time to argue. He gave her a searching look, before letting out the clutch and continuing on their way.

* * *

James was comfortably installed in a modern four-bedded ward at the hospital, his bed positioned next to the window, which gave him a panoramic view of the city. He looked more rested and less frightened than he had earlier when in casualty, and he beamed crookedly when he saw them.

''Lo,' he managed, and Gina's heart soared as she realised his speech was returning.

'Hello, Dad.' She kissed his pale cheek. 'Feeling a little better?'

He nodded, and Jude pulled up two chairs for them to sit down.

'Now, you're not to worry about a thing.' Jude's capable voice inspired confidence. 'Gina and I are managing just fine.'

James gave his daughter an enquiring

look, and she forced herself to smile her agreement.

'Yes,' Jude went on relentlessly, 'we're forming quite a tight partnership, aren't we Gina?'

Count to ten, Gina, count to ten, she thought.

'Yes, quite,' she said, but her eyes when she turned her back on her father to face her tormentor said something very different.

They didn't stay long. It was still early days for James, and the ward sister advised them not to tire him, but it had been long enough for Jude to force his advantage and convince the choreographer that a separate business administrator was a good idea.

'So, I'll go ahead and draw up the partnership papers, shall I?' Jude suggested, and James nodded, while Gina seethed on the sidelines.

'Of all the sly, underhand schemes — ' she began when they were on their own in the lift on the way down, but he cut her short.

'Rubbish! As I told you, James asked me to join the company this morning and I accepted. I'm simply putting everything on a formal footing.'

'I thought we weren't going to worry Dad with business?'

'Nor are we. That's why I have to be a legal partner, so that I don't have to go running to him for the OK whenever a problem arises.'

Her bitter laugh proved she was unconvinced.

'So you can make all the decisions, you mean. What's your first change going to be — getting the dancers to advertise products on their costumes, like sportsmen do?'

He looked her up and down.

'Actually, that's not such a bad idea,' he drawled, and strode ahead to the car.

9

The following weeks proved difficult ones for Gina. Although he was making good progress, she continued to worry about her father, and the little flat seemed horribly empty without him.

Work was a different problem; she wished she were alone there, or at least, that the new administrator would go away. Seeing him every day did not improve her temper, nor, if she were truthful about it, the aching void which his betrayal had left in her heart.

For she was discovering that it was impossible to turn passion on and off like a tap, and in spite of the fact that she now saw Jude in his true colours, she was quite unable to turn off the desire he had awakened within her. How unfair life was — that when she finally had found the one man who could put the lie to David's taunts, whose very touch brought her alive, he should turn out to be just another user.

It didn't help that Jude was making such a great job of running the Eastern, either. She knew it was only her pride that was hurt, but when the rest of the company chatted about his efficiency and the excellent changes he was bringing in, she wanted to scream. One of his instigations was a weekly meeting on stage before rehearsals on a Friday morning, when he explained his future plans and invited suggestions from the floor. It was a popular move, keeping the company informed and making them feel intimately involved in the rescue operation, and on her good days, Gina was prepared to admit it was a sensible idea.

What made her furious, however, was when Jude announced new initiatives without any reference to her. It was as if he didn't think her opinion worth listening to, and she was sure he was purposely snubbing her.

'Right — good morning, everyone.'

He strode on stage, immaculately suited. One thing he had made very clear from his first day was that business was business, and just because he was now in the entertainment industry, he did not intend to let his standards slip. So he continued to dress formally, and expected those of his employees who were in customer contact positions to do the same.

The sight of his powerful body as he stood on the rostrum sent a small shiver of memory zipping down Gina's spine. Surrounding him were some of the most highly trained male dancers in England, yet beside his athletic frame they appeared, to her eyes at least, also-rans. Jude did not carry a pound of surplus weight, and as he stood poised to speak, he reminded her of a leopard waiting to pounce.

He must be tremendously fit to bear such favourable comparison to the professionals, she thought, and wondered if he worked out. He probably had his own gym, and she was overcome by a wave of disappointment that she would never be in a position to find out for sure.

'First the good news,' Jude began. 'Following on from a suggestion by Georgina, I have approached a number of companies for sponsorship.' Gina's ears pricked up, and she wondered what he, meant. Then she remembered her facetious suggestion about advertising, and saw he was teasing her. She cast him an angry look, but he didn't seem to notice. 'So far, two banks, an insurance company and an airline have come on board, and I'm hoping for more. Also, I'm applying to the Arts Council for funding. I know they've been cutting their grants, but as we have never asked before, I think we might be lucky.'

Gina felt her hackles rising as she noted the way everyone hung onto Jude's words. She knew it was only sour grapes on her part, and that she ought to be delighted that for the first time in months the Eastern was not financially embarrassed, but she was not that altruistic.

Jude made it all sound so simple, and perhaps for him with his business background, it was. But for her it had been a never-ending battle to keep their heads above water, and she resented the ease with which he had managed to reverse their fortunes. As much as anything, she felt it reflected badly on her administration — as if she should have been able to run things better herself.

'Now for the bad news.' Jude held up his hands to silence the chatter. 'Well, not bad, exactly, it just might be a slight shock to some of you. You may know that when the Eastern was first founded, it was a touring company because it had no home base. This theatre wasn't ready for a number of years, and even when it was completed, the greater part of the year was spent touring. It's only in recent times that policy changed, and quite frankly, it's not working. The theatre's not large enough to support a long season in Branchester, and we're going to have to get back on the road, with just a limited season here.'

Amid the frenzied questions and discussions, Gina felt out on a limb. While the majority of the company seemed excited by the prospect of touring, she alone was subdued. But then, it was her parents' policy that had been criticised, and she could not expect to enjoy Jude faulting them in public.

She followed him back to the office — she refused to call it his — and turned on him.

'How dare you implement all these changes without consulting me?' she demanded. 'It is my father's company, after all!'

He regarded her without a ripple on his mask-like face.

'Yes, your *father's* company,' he emphasised, 'not yours. Why should I consult you?'

She gave him a glacial stare. He knew exactly how to rile her, and she wondered if he did so on purpose. He was so frighteningly self-contained that she longed to be able to breakthrough his iron control and make him lose his temper, however nerve-racking it was to be on the receiving end of it. Anything would be preferable to his present studied indifference.

'Because Dad isn't in any fit state to make the decisions himself.'

'Exactly, which is why I make them on his behalf. That's what partners are for, to cover for each other if ever one is incapacitated.'

She turned on him, eyes glinting furiously, as much at his icy calmness as at what he had done. It seemed as if it was impossible to outsmart him, and she longed to be able to puncture his practised reserve.

'This idea of touring — you know very well Dad won't be up to it for ages, and I certainly couldn't leave him alone at Boundary Road. That means you'd be without a ballerina after Alicia retires this year.'

'I'm glad to hear of your devotion to James — it does you credit. I'm not so sure he'd be pleased to hear of your decision to nursemaid him, however.'

'Well, I'm sure he'll be very grateful to hear how well the Eastern is doing with your help,' she said, dripping sarcasm. 'On the other hand, he might take exception to his policies being criticised in front of the whole company.'

His face was impassive.

'Don't be silly, Gina, there's nothing personal on this. James wants the company to survive, and I'm doing my best to ensure that it does.'

'By ridiculing him in front of his employees?'

'I was not aware that I had ridiculed anyone. However, if you wish to overreact to everything I do — '

'Overreact? You force your way into this company, make changes without a by-your-leave, act as if you own the place — and then have the nerve to say I'm overreacting!' She was bristling with rage and turned to leave.

'Would you rather I simply let the Eastern fail?' he asked, a grim expression on his face. 'It would destroy all the work your parents put in and throw many people out of work, but at least you could feel you'd kept face. Because that's what all this is about, isn't it? You don't like the fact that you are no longer in control.'

His assessment of the situation infuriated her, and she swung round angrily.

'Oh, that's rich, coming from you! You've been trying to muscle your way into the Eastern for months, and now that you've succeeded, you're enjoying throwing your weight around. Well, your domineering attitude doesn't impress me, at all!'

'No?' He moved towards her, his face taut. 'I used to be able to impress you — you thought better of me once. What made you change your mind?'

She looked away. He seemed disturbingly tall and strong and she knew if she stayed to exchange words with him, he would be the winner — he was impossible to outwit. She dropped her eyes under his penetrating gaze, and her heart began to pound uncomfortably. So he still had the power to excite her — his nearness continued to speak to some primitive need deep within her body. She hated herself for such weakness, but knew the only way to combat such physical attraction was to avoid her tormentor.

'You tricked me to get an entrée here,' Gina stuck her chin out defiantly, 'and whatever you say, I'm sure you've got an ulterior motive for wanting to join us!'

His face flushed a dangerous deep red, and he gripped his hands together as he stared intently at her ashen complexion. Yet he did not deny her accusation, and she had the strangest feeling that she had scored a hit.

'You are, of course, entitled to your opinion,' was all he said, before turning away from her and examining some papers on his desk.

She left the office deep in thought. What was Jude's real reason for bailing out the Eastern — and why was he so determined to call the tune? She knew there were certain men who hated having their judgment questioned, but there was more to it than that. She shook her head, and determined to get to the bottom of the mystery.

'Gina!' Madame Berthe hailed the girl as she made for the foyer. 'Just a minute please, I want to talk to you.'

'Yes, Madame?'

'My dear child, I have a confession to make.' The ballet mistress steered her towards a private corner. 'I have wanted to tell you for some time, but you've always looked so fierce whenever I've broached the subject that I really have been rather nervous.'

'Really?' Gina was intrigued. What could Madame Berthe mean?

'Yes, it's about Jude Alexander.' She saw the girl stiffen and hurried on. 'Well, more about me, really. You're wronging him, you know. You see, it wasn't he who told your father you were skipping classes, it was I.'

'You? But why?'

Madame Berthe shrugged eloquently.

'Gina, child, I had to! Your dancing was going downhill, and you were not open to reason! Whenever I approached you on the subject you said you had too much office work to do, so I decided to tackle James.'

Gina cast her mind back and remembered Madame Berthe's concern. If it had been she who had gone to James, it was no wonder he had been worried. He valued the ballet mistress's opinion on all things, but especially on the progress of members of the company. That his own daughter was playing hooky would have appalled him, and if it had been hinted that he was to blame for driving her too hard, he would have been even more distressed. She frowned, finding it hard to accept that her father's worries might not have been caused by Jude at all — but then she recalled Mr Lindt's remark in her dressing-room that he and the businessman had been discussing finance with James that afternoon, and she knew she need not reproach herself. Jude had been stalking James for weeks.

'Well, I did suspect Jude, it's true, but even if it wasn't him, I know he's been harassing Dad to let him become a partner in the company.'

'Harassing? That's rather strong, isn't it? And he was offering a lot in return — '

'His *business expertise*, you mean? Oh, I know all about that! We're having it shoved down our throats every Friday.'

'Gina, my dear, don't be a goose! There is something rather pompous about people who insist on sneering at the commercial theatre as if it were in some way tainted. There is no special merit in starving in a garret for Art with a capital A, you know!'

Gina blushed. She knew what Madame Berthe said was true, but she refused to admit Jude was blameless. He did have some special reason for wanting to join them, she knew it, and was determined to find out what it was.

'What exactly did you say to Dad?' she asked.

'Simply that you were doing too much, and that the company needed a financial director.'

'You said that?'

The ballet mistress nodded, quite unrepentant. 'Yes, and I even went so far as to suggest Mr Alexander.'

'What? Why?' Gina raised her voice in amazement.

'Shh, there's no need to shout. I said to James that he could do a lot worse than invite Jude Alexander to join the company. I did it to protect the Eastern and to protect you. You are a truly talented dancer and I couldn't bear to see you throw your gift away.'

Gina gasped. So Jude had been speaking the truth when he claimed James had asked him. She had not liked to broach the subject with her father in his present state; she knew that he was relieved when Jude had told him they were working together, but had remained unconvinced James had suggested a partnership in the first place. Now it looked as if she had been mistaken.

'I wasn't aware that you knew Mr Alexander that well.' Her voice was shaky after the shock she had received.

'I met him at a reception some months ago. He seemed very knowledgeable about ballet — he mentioned he thought your dancing was slipping, and I told him about our problems. He was most interested and said he wanted to diversify into the arts, so I suggested he contacted James.'

So it was Madame Berthe who had put Jude up to it! Gina shook her head. She wondered when he had seen her dance previously, and hoped it was in one of her triumphs . . .

She gave herself a mental shake — why should she care whether he had thought her good or bad? His opinion was of no interest to her any more. Madame Berthe might have sown the seed, but it was Jude who had hounded her father until he agreed terms — and for some months, according to the ballet mistress — and for the stress he had caused her father, she could never forgive him.

'Thank you for telling me.' She gave a strained smile. 'I'm just off to see Dad now — shall I give him your love?'

'Yes, do. And Gina, *ma petite*, am I forgiven?'

'Of course.' Gina kissed the ballet mistress's cheek to prove it.

★ ★ ★

She stopped off at the local newsagent on the way, wanting to get chocolates and magazines for her father. James had made excellent progress since his stroke, and hoped to be home fairly soon. He could walk with the aid of a stick now, his right foot dragging only slightly, and his speech was almost back to normal, with just the faintest trace of slurring in his words. Gina had nothing but praise for the hospital staff.

'Hello, Sister Powell.' She nodded as that frighteningly efficient young woman swept by. 'How's my father today?'

'Doing very well.' The slight figure in navy blue smiled pleasantly. 'He'll soon be back home, but I want you to promise me you'll make sure he doesn't start smoking again.'

'Dad's always been a smoker — '

'And it almost killed him. I think we'd better have a talk. Come into, my office a minute, will you?'

Gina followed her into the small staff-room, and sat in the empty chair indicated. Sister Powell sat at her desk and leaned forward, elbows on table with hands clasped.

'Gina, do you know anything about what caused your father's stroke?' she asked.

'Oh, yes.' Gina could not hide the bitterness in her voice. 'It was stress, no doubt about it.'

'Stress is only indirectly linked to stroke, because it may increase blood

252

pressure, but it has to be long term, unresolved stress. Was that what your father had?'

'No.' Honestly forbade Gina from pretending that Jude's offer had been very long in the pipeline — a few months at most.

'No,' the young nurse went on, 'I thought not. But what is very often to blame is smoking. Was Mr George a heavy smoker?' and at Gina's nod, 'Yes, he said so himself. Well, it's no more cigarettes for him from now on — not if he wants to avoid another stroke.'

Gina stood up to leave. As she reached the door, she turned back — she had to be sure.

'Stress really had nothing to do with it?'

'In view of the amount your father smoked, I'd say very little indeed.'

She wandered into her father's ward, thoughts miles away.

'Gina, Swan Princess,' her father greeted her with delight. 'How are you?'

'I'm fine. Dad, have you given up smoking?'

He grimaced. 'Oh, yes. I still get terrible cravings, but they tell me they'll pass. Can't risk another stroke though, can I?'

She shook her head. What a fool she had been! She had jumped to conclusions without any evidence, and by her own stupidity had ruined the most successful relationship she had ever experienced.

Or had she? What if she went to Jude and apologised . . . would he forgive her, or would he throw her words of remorse back in her face? She trembled as she imagined the anger he might display, but knew she would have to risk his wrath — not only because she had been unjust, but also because she wanted him back so very much.

She had missed his closeness horribly. What was his magic that after only a few dates she should be so ensnared? She doubted she could ever feel for another what she had felt for him. It was as if they had been made for each other, and she thought it extremely unlikely she would meet such a kindred spirit again.

But would he take her back? There was only one way to find out.

She dragged her thoughts back to the present. James was anxious to hear about the company.

'You know Jude wants to get us back touring?' she asked.

He nodded, his eyes looking excited by the prospect. 'Yes, and I think it's an excellent idea! Taking ballet to the people like Pavlova did — that's what it's all about really. It always was our policy, but circumstances intervened . . . ' He trailed off.

Suddenly, she had to know.

'Dad, do you like Jude Alexander?'

He watched her closely as he replied.

'Yes, I do. He's absolutely straight, and I like that in a man. I trust him implicitly.'

'You don't think he has some ulterior motive for wanting to join us?'

Again that watchful look. Then, 'I have no reason to guess so.'

255

'I'm probably just being silly —'

'Swan Princess, one day you are going to have to learn to trust again.'

She gave a start. Rarely did her father discuss her private life.

'I know David hurt you, but look at the man he was. There is no comparison to Jude.'

She sucked her lips inwards as if trying to distribute newly applied lipstick evenly, her normal warning sign not to pry.

'I know you didn't like David,' she said. 'Why did you take him on — just to humour me?'

'Not to humour you, to help you. I knew you had a difficult time ahead, and thought he could support you through it. Foolish, really, for that young man very quickly showed his true colours, to me at least, and the last thing he was interested in was helping others.'

'What do you mean? What difficult time?'

James George sighed, and for once looked his age and more. 'Your mother.

You remember the two of us went out without you in London that last summer?' When she nodded, he continued, 'Well, we were visiting specialists. Marjory had cancer, you see, and we hoped to find someone who could arrest the disease.'

Gina's eye flew wide with shock. Her mother had been dreadfully ill and she had not known.

'Why didn't you tell me?'

'It was her decision, Princess. You know her favourite saying, 'don't anticipate sorrow', and she wanted to save you from worrying until the last possible moment. We meant to tell you eventually, but then the car crash changed everything.'

'Poor, darling Mum.' Gina's throat stung with swallowed tears.

'No, it was better that way . . . no awful lingering. She had hoped to live to see the première of *Anna Karenina*, but it was not to be.'

'Thank heavens! Oh, Dad, I don't mean it like it sounds, but I would have hated her to see that disaster! Now I feel even more guilty about it, because if you hadn't been trying to protect me, you wouldn't have engaged David, and Anthony May would have danced the part of Vronsky so much better.'

'It's all water under the bridge now, darling, and I've said before that you shouldn't blame yourself.'

Easy to say, she thought, *impossible not to.*

'How long had Mum known?'

'That she had cancer? Four years. That was why we stopped touring — she needed to be in one place for treatment, and the constant travelling exhausted her. You were too young to understand at first, and then the right moment to tell you never seemed to arise.'

Gina went to the huge window and stared over Branchester. It was a wonderful day and the view was terrific. Spread out around her was the enchanting city: the busy streets and brightly striped awnings of the market, the gleaming spires of many churches, the shimmering thread of the river, and solemnly standing guard over them all, the majestic castle.

Up until today she would have said she was a fairly observant sort of person, yet she had just discovered that for four years her mother had been fighting for her life, and she had been unaware of the fact. She found it incredible, and wondered what else in life she had missed.

'Dad.' She rested her weight on the side of his bed. 'Did Jude discuss the company's financial situation with you?'

He nodded. 'When I brought the subject up, he did. He was most reluctant to talk money at all initially — I think he thought I might be shocked — but once he realised I knew the hole we are in, he proved most helpful.'

'You knew! How?'

He gave her a guilty glance. 'Oh, I kept my eyes open. I know you like to think of me as some kind of recalcitrant schoolboy, but I needed to know how things were going, so I used to pop into

259

the office when you weren't there. Don't forget, I had to help Marjory when she became ill and even after she died. It was really only after *Karenina* that you took over so completely.'

She blushed uneasily, remembering Jude's accusation that she smothered her father.

'Why didn't you tell me I was patronising you?'

James shifted forward on the bed and slipped his left arm unsteadily round her shoulders.

'You didn't mean to, Swan Princess — and I thought you liked doing the books to keep your mind off David's desertion, so I decided not to interfere.'

'You *thought* I *liked* doing them?' She clapped her palm to her forehead. 'I hated all the admin work. What about you?'

'Me too.' He gave an impish grin. 'By the time of the première I knew I'd have to get someone in to help, but then you took over and I didn't want to upset you.'

'Even though I was doing so badly?'

He looked rather sheepish. 'Well, I did think I'd have to muscle in when Berthe told me you'd been skipping classes, blaming me for forcing you to do all that paperwork! Don't forget, you're an outstanding dancer and only an indifferent administrator, so it seemed crazy to sacrifice your talent to a ledger!'

'Not to mention sacrificing the company to my maladministration?' she enquired, but her father only chuckled.

'You weren't that bad,' he said. 'Nearly, but not quite!'

They were still enjoying the joke when the bell rang to herald the end of visiting hours, and Gina kissed her father.

'I won't miss class any more, Dad,' she promised, and he patted her hand.

'Good. And you don't resent my asking Jude to become a partner?'

She shook her head, and after a concerted effort, James managed to give her a wink goodbye.

★ ★ ★

On the bus on the return journey, Gina considered all that her father had told her. A lot of things fell into place now that she knew how unwell her mother had been towards the end of her life — the mountain of unfinished paperwork she had left behind, so unlike the methodical Marjory; her distracted air at rehearsals for *Karenina*; David's forgotten contract; it all added up.

Gina was flabbergasted by her own lack of observation, but she realised she had been heavily involved with David at the time, and thus well-versed in the gentle art of self-deception. Perhaps she had extended the practice to cover her mother's condition; she did remember Marjory being paler and more tired than usual as they prepared for the première of the new ballet.

She wondered if she were any more observant today, and decided she was. Indeed, if her suspicions about Jude Alexander were anything to go by, it would seem she now veered too far in the opposite direction, for she had doubted his motives from the moment they met, and even after she had softened her attitude towards him, she still had felt he had some secret reason for wanting the Eastern.

But then, she had met him after her experience with David had taught her to be wary in relationships. She would have to say sorry — but would he be prepared to listen?

She looked out of the window as the bus rounded the castle, and caught sight of him talking to someone in the street. What a coincidence . . . or was it? If she were truthful, she found her thoughts turning to him almost every moment of the day; it would be more of a coincidence for her to come upon him when he was not on her mind.

She wondered if he would accept her apology — she had to admit she didn't relish facing him — but the longer she put it off, the more difficult it would become.

Strike while the iron's hot, she thought recklessly, and rose to disembark at the next stop. She stared intently as the bus swept past the two men, and found there was something vaguely familiar about the second one who had his back to her. She craned her neck to get a clearer view, and as he turned out of the breeze to light a cigarette, she was startled to recognise Stan.

What on earth was Jude doing with him? she wondered. Surely he had been only too glad to see the back of him? The two men seemed to be having an intense conversation, and she itched to know what it was about, yet suddenly got the impression they would not appreciate being disturbed.

She was not sure how she knew — something about their huddled positions and the almost furtive way Stan was glancing around as if checking no-one could see him — and she decided not to interrupt them.

Instead she climbed off the bus and

cut through the arcade on her way home. It was a lovely day for a walk, and she experienced an overwhelming sense of relief that she had decided not to tackle Jude. He had called her a coward once before, and she had to agree with his description, but both men had looked particularly fierce, and she was glad she had not got involved.

She hoped Stan did not intend to try and make trouble for the Eastern — but would he dare, now that he had Jude to contend with?

Suddenly she laughed, and, 'Not my problem any more!' she exclaimed. A passing shopper gave her a very old-fashioned look which left no doubt as to what he thought of people who talked to themselves, and Gina giggled as she continued on her way.

She remembered Jude's song of praise to Branchester, and for the first time realised she felt just the same about the place. She loved the historic buildings and winding streets of the old city, and was glad so much of it had been preserved for posterity. If the company did revert to lengthy tours, she would always look forward to returning to her East Anglian home.

★   ★   ★

That evening Gina was dancing in *Les Sylphides* again, and as she donned the airy tarlatan dress, she reflected how her life had changed in the past two years. She had discovered romance, learned a deep truth about her father, and most important of all, had become a complete person.

She gave a dry smile. It was called maturing, and though she was aware no experience in life was wasted, she knew that to her, the most momentous occasion of all had been meeting Jude.

'Overture and beginners, please.'

She rose to the command and climbed the stairs as Chopin's lyrical music filled the air. She fidgeted in the wings as the overture played, pressing the toes and soles of her ballet shoes in the resin box by the prompt corner to prevent them from slipping, and fiddling with the circlet of flowers round her head. She always felt the same way while awaiting her cue; nervous, tense and excited, and she stared blankly at the darkened stage until the curtains swished apart and she stepped into the magical world of the ballet.

Les Sylphides had no storyline as such; a poet searching for inspiration comes upon a ghostly glade where sylphs dance in the moonlight against the backdrop of a ruined monastery. This lack of a plot did not make it an easy option, however, with the dancers' performances standing or falling on their ability to produce a delicacy of style and technical accomplishment of the highest order.

It relied upon smooth, fluid lines, inbuilt musicality and expressive nuance to arrive at the right fragility of atmosphere, and the Eastern dancers were considered among the greatest exponents of the masterpiece.

Gina danced with the joy of dancing.

Just as people climbed mountains because they were there, so she danced because she felt compelled. She bounded, she spun, she captivated with the purity of her line and the thrust of her attack. As the curtains swung to a close, the appreciative applause and stamping of feet told her she had succeeded, just for a moment, in suspending belief so that the audience, too, believed in magic.

She felt elated and tired as she staggered back to her dressing-room, bouquets in hand. She admired a sheath of lilies and carnations — an unusual combination, she thought, though not the one she particularly wanted. The red roses had stopped arriving the day of her father's stroke. After all she had said to him, she could not blame Jude — and indeed, had been delighted by their disappearance at first, though now she longed for just one stem from him.

'Miss George.' The voice was curt, but she did not mind. It was better than not hearing it at all.

'Yes?' She turned and saw him

walking towards her.

'I would be grateful if you would join us in the royal box as soon as you are changed.'

He might have worded it as a request — but his tone left no doubt but that it was an order.

'Fine.' She smiled and licked her lips nervously before she continued, 'Actually, I was wondering if I might talk to you some time — in private — it's rather important — ' She broke off as she recognised ill-veiled impatience in the hard-boned face.

'Some other time.' He dismissed her request coldly. 'I'm busy tonight.'

She watched his departing figure feeling sadly deflated. She had not supposed it would be easy to apologise, or that he would jump at the chance of talking to her, but she had hoped he might be a little more forgiving.

She shrugged. She would simply have to try later when he had not so much on his mind.

She changed quickly, pulling on the

jeans and blouse she had worn that day. She wiped her face clean of make-up, and headed for the royal box.

The name was an old joke — there were only two boxes in the auditorium at the Little, and both of them became cramped if more than four people crushed into them. The idea that any member of the royal family might condescend to sit in such discomfort was quite ridiculous. James had playfully nicknamed them the royal and the regal, and the names had stuck.

She paused outside the door to the royal and debated whether to knock or not. For all that she knew she had wronged him, it went against the grain to request permission to enter any part of the theatre that she had known as hers since childhood, but good manners won the day.

'Come!' His voice was overconfident and set her teeth on edge.

She walked in and saw he was not alone. As her eyes became accustomed to the dimmed lighting, she recognised the girl seated next to him.

'Ah, Miss George.' Jude rose to his feet and helped her to a vacant chair. 'I don't believe you've met Angelica Clarke, have you?'

'No,' Gina shook her head slowly, 'but I know about you, of course. You were with the Scottish Ballet, weren't you? I saw you in their production of *Napoli*.'

The blonde smiled. 'That's right. I left them a couple of years ago for a fixed term contract in Paris which has just ended, so I'm footloose and fancy free. At least, I was until I spoke to Jude this evening. There I was, all set for a pleasant country weekend with an old friend, and what do I find but that he's bought a ballet company! Not only that, but he offers me the position of ballerina with the great James George as choreographer!'

Gina was glad she was sitting down; the news had made her feel weak, and she doubted she could have remained standing. Her colour ebbed and flowed as she tried to control the jealousy and hurt that threatened to choke her. She felt betrayed all over again. At last she knew why Jude had wanted a partnership in the Eastern — as a showcase for his dancing girlfriend.

'When will you be joining us?' she asked dully, her heart heavy with rejection.

'Almost immediately. Jude can be very persuasive.' Angelica leaned forward and touched the tip of his nose with her finger. It was an oddly intimate gesture, and caused a lump to catch in Gina's throat. Angelica was a glamorous woman, with sleek blonde hair and deep-set grey eyes, and her sojourn in France had clearly introduced her to the legendary Gallic chic.

'I'd better go now.' Gina was saved by the dimming of the house lights for the next one act ballet. 'Nice to meet you.' She felt dowdy and provincial in comparison to the elegant newcomer, and just wanted to beat her retreat.

She stumbled out of the box and

clattered down the uncarpeted stone stairs to the emergency exit. It was humid and oppressively hot outside; it had been forecast that the unseasonable heat wave was about to break and return to more usual late spring weather, and it certainly felt that way. She shoved her hands deep into her trouser pockets and walked away, wanting to get as far as possible from the theatre.

She trudged along, head down, looking neither to left nor right, travelling as if directed by remote control. A flash of lightning raced across the sky, swiftly followed by a crack of thunder and torrential rain. She was soon soaked, her wet jeans rubbing her thighs and her shoes squelching with every step. She barely noticed the purr of an engine as a car pulled in beside her.

'You look like a drowned rat. Get in the car and I'll run you home.'

She was too relieved to argue, and as she slid inside, the warmth of the Porsche enveloped her. Her clothes stuck to her so she felt cold and clammy, and her hair dripped in small trickles down her neck and back.

'Here, have this.' He removed his jacket and wrapped it around her. 'What on earth possessed you to venture out in this weather?'

'I wanted to get home,' she lied, then shivered. She was feeling distinctly feverish herself, though whether because of his proximity of because she had a cold coming on, she couldn't say.

'Why didn't you get a taxi? In fact, why didn't you ask me to give you a lift?'

She gave a petulant toss of the head. 'I thought you'd be with Angelica.'

He seemed not to notice her sour expression. 'No, I had to stay on late to do some work, so my driver took her back to Melrose.'

'Well, I didn't know that and I didn't want to disturb you. I expect you have a great deal to discuss with her — it's not every day the Eastern gets a new ballerina.'

The acidic tone of her voice gave her

away, and he flashed her an enquiring look.

'What's eating you?' he asked. 'Don't you approve of my choice?'

'Oh, Angelica's a good dancer.' Gina's fair-mindedness would not let her run her rival down. 'But who says we need another principal, and on whose authority did you decide to employ her?'

'Mine. You forget, I'm a partner now.'

'Well, I don't know that we need her.'

I certainly don't, thought Gina, but she suspected Jude was only to keen to welcome the other girl into the bosom of the Eastern.

'So that's what you're going on about — jealousy,' he said, and Gina froze.

She hated to admit it, but he was right; she could not bear to think of Angelica enjoying the kisses she had thought were hers. A violent wave of resentment rushed through her, against this man who had awoken a great need within her only to leave her cruelly unfulfilled.

'Rubbish!' she snapped, for she could

not bear him to know how she felt. But she need not have worried, for his next sentence proved he was thinking of something entirely different . . .

'No, it's not — you are jealous. You don't like the thought of competition from another young ballerina.'

There was some truth in what he said, Gina had to admit. She did hold a rather proprietorial air about the company, but it was understandable given that her parents had founded the Eastern. Nowadays, however, she had to remember it was not just her father who made the decisions — indeed, since his stroke, Jude seemed to be the one calling the tune.

'I don't think you had any right to hire Angelica without asking James first,' she persisted.

He gave an exasperated hiss as he let out air between his teeth. 'It seems I can't win with you!' he said in a thunderous voice. 'One minute you're accusing me of worrying your father, the next you're furious that I don't run to him with every little detail. There was no big deal about hiring Angelica — we need a new ballerina.'

'Says who?' Gina demanded.

'You, for one. Don't you remember? You said you would have to stay at home to care for James and wouldn't be able to come on tour. Well, with Alicia retiring at the end of the season, it seemed like a good idea to fill the post now.'

His words rather took the wind out of her sails. Why did he always have to sound so reasonable? It was true, of course, Alicia was leaving soon, and Gina had refused to go on tour.

The problem was she now recognised that part of her refusal was out of loyalty to James, feeling he had been used by Jude; once she knew her father approved of the tour, she wished she could reverse the decision.

She sneezed. The slapping of the windscreen wipers beat in time to the pulse pounding inside her head. She felt cold and lost and miserable. And alone — terribly, terribly alone. In spite of the nearness to her of the man she loved.

She gasped, the implication of the admission from her subconscious mind striking her forcibly. He gave her a quick, quizzical look before returning his attention to the road, and she battled to control her facial muscles, determined not to give herself away.

Of course she loved him — had done almost since the day they had met — the chemistry between them should have told her that. Yet she had attempted to explain it away, putting her intoxicated behaviour down to mere physical attraction — Jude was very attractive, after all — when all the time she had fallen deeply and completely in love.

She should have known her body would not play her false — she had never responded to David in the same way as her senses sang to Jude's embrace, and it was just so much foolishness to try and pretend otherwise.

Why had she been so insistent on

ignoring the tell-tale signs — was it fear of a second desertion? She assumed so; she had not loved David, she now realised, yet still it had hurt her when he left; subconsciously she must have been aware how very much worse would be Jude's rejection.

And it was. Real loss, she was discovering, was akin to fear — the tightening bands of pain in her chest and the stabs of worry that tormented her proved that. But she would not let him see; must not feed his ego with the knowledge of her captive heart.

Oh, it would be hard watching him with Angelica, knowing that once she had thought it might have been her he wanted — but she would survive. No one died of a broken heart, after all, though love itself could shrivel and die if left untended. But hers would not.

Though she didn't intend to become a latter-day Miss Havisham, sitting in her wedding finery awaiting the groom who never came, she knew as surely as she knew herself, that Jude was the only man for her. She would never love another as she loved him.

'I hope this weather doesn't last,' he said. 'We'll all get so wet travelling between the theatre and Boundary Road that we're sure to go down with colds. It's a nuisance the school isn't nearer the theatre.'

He looked at her as if inviting comment, but she was saved from making a reply as they had arrived at their destination, and she tensed herself to jump out.

'You should have a hot bath and go straight to bed,' he suggested, 'though I have no doubt it's too late to stop you catching something.'

'Thanks for your concern.'

She opened the car door, slammed it behind her and sprinted for the house.

10

Unfortunately, Jude's prophecy came true, and after struggling to carry on with a cold, Gina finally gave in and went to bed for twenty-four hours.

Probably another day in the warm would have been sensible, but when Friday dawned, she was determined to go to the theatre and hear what other changes for the company the new partner was cooking. She dragged herself out of bed and surveyed her reflection in the mirror.

She didn't look well. Her complexion was pale and she had dark bags under her eyes, while the eyes themselves were puffy and red and her nose was an unlovely shade of pink. The overall picture was not very fetching. Still, even before the cold she had been unable to compete with Angelica's glamour — and she knew that was why her appearance should suddenly concern her — for the new ballerina looked a million dollars, making Gina feel faded and drawn in comparison.

She was greeted by friendly calls when she walked on stage at the theatre, and was so busy assuring everyone that she felt much better, she didn't notice Jude arrive.

'When Miss George deigns to pay attention, I'll begin!' He eyed her distantly, cool impatience in his expression.

She flushed sharply. There was no need for him to display his hostility so openly — surely he didn't enjoy humiliating her? His next announcement answered that question.

'I'm reviving *Anna Karenina*. It'll open at the end of the season here, and then we'll take it on tour. Alicia, Georgina and Angelica will share the title role.'

He had dropped a bombshell, and the company was not entirely sure how to take it. *Karenina* had been such a failure that some of, them clearly doubted the wisdom of its resurrection, while others were excited by the thought of a second chance.

Gina was not among their number, and noticed she was receiving some searching looks — the dancers were anxious to know how she was taking the news. She tried hard to appear blasé.

Inside she was simmering with rage. What did he want to do — make her look a fool in front of the whole company? Or perhaps there was more to it than that, and he wanted her to appear ridiculous on stage?

For if she was to alternate the role with Angelica, what better way for him to build up his new girlfriend than that she should follow a performance which he knew the critics had already slated? Anna was not Gina's kind of role, and she was as sure as he must be that her interpretation would be lacklustre, a fact she pointed out to him immediately after the meeting.

'I won't dance it!' she declared. 'You're only doing this to make me look a fool.'

A frown creased his forehead.

'Not more histrionics, please, Gina. Surely even you can't be so conceited as to imagine I would go to the expense of re-staging a ballet just to annoy you!'

'You know that it was a complete fiasco — '

'Yes, was, past tense. It's not going to be this time.'

'How can you be so sure?' she demanded. 'Have you bought the critics, like you buy everyone else?'

He shot her a hard look.

'We won't have that poser David Bryant trying to hog the ballet, for a start — added to which all three ballerinas will be well-rehearsed, experienced women.' He stressed the word experienced.

'Is that why you made love to me — to prepare me for the role?'

She knew it had to be true, and felt a terrible sadness as she accepted his kisses and soft words had been nothing more than a calculated manoeuvre on his part. She turned and saw the fury on his face.

'How dare you accuse me of such behaviour?' He strode up to her. 'We were together because we were attracted to each other, because it was what we both wanted, and don't you dare try and say otherwise!'

With that he forced his lips upon hers, bruising her with his assault. It was not the kind of kiss he had taught her to appreciate — those had been gentle and giving — this was hard and brutal, as if he would force her to admit their previous encounters had meant something.

Suddenly he broke free.

'Have I made my point? You wanted me as much as I wanted you — *Karenina* had nothing to do with it.'

In spite of his forceful approach, waves of excitement had shot through Gina while Jude was kissing her. Now she was ashamed of her reaction, sure that Jude was only humouring her.

'So you won't drop *Karenina*?'

'My mind is made up.' His voice was clipped and she knew she had lost.

If she had thought her father might

support her, she was to be disillusioned there, too. James was delighted that his ballet was to be revived.

'I don't think I'd have been brave enough to do it myself, Swan Princess, but I'm glad he is.'

'He wants me to dance Anna.'

She expected her father to protest.

'Excellent!' he exclaimed. 'You've matured since the première and will do well.'

She stared at him, dumbfounded.

'But Dad, you always said you should never have let me dance Anna.'

'Nor should I with that cocky young man,' James said. 'You were just blooming, and it was cruel to let him smash your confidence like that. But when Alicia had to pull out I was at my wits' end, and felt I didn't have any choice. I did, of course — I should have cancelled the première rather than let him use you that way. He ruined your performance, which was tragic as you were so very good as Anna.'

'You mean it wasn't my fault that

Karenina failed?' Gina couldn't believe what she was hearing.

'Your fault? Of course not! Gina, you haven't been carrying round the idea that it was for all this time?' And when she nodded, 'Oh, Swan Princess, what a fool I've been — I didn't know.'

'But the papers said — '

'That you were too young to control your partner, which you were. They were on your side, Swan Princess, and attached the blame to David. Didn't you understand that?'

She shook her head. In her misery, she had been too despondent to do anything but take the headlines at face value.

A thought struck her. 'But what if I fail again?'

'You didn't fail last time, darling, and now you have a second chance to show just what you are capable of.'

Gina realised her father was right — and even if Jude Alexander was only putting on the ballet as a showcase for Angelica, still she would seize the

287

opportunity with both hands and embrace the role of Anna.

★ ★ ★

'You're doing well,' Jude told her some weeks later at rehearsal. 'What made you change your mind about *Karenina*?'

'My father,' she said shortly. 'He was so pleased about the revival. He was very hurt by the flop and I saw how he wanted that failure to be rectified.'

'Yes — you weren't thinking of others.' He didn't mince his words. 'Also Alicia was longing to get a crack at the role she just missed dancing last time. Anna was created for her, when all's said and done, and it'll be a wonderful finale to a distinguished career.'

Gina flushed. 'You're a fine one to talk about being selfish! What's more selfish than hijacking the Eastern just to impress a ballerina?'

His face was grim. 'So you finally understand?'

'I don't need it spelling out to me!'

Her heart was heavy as she walked away. It was one thing to guess the reason Jude had wanted the company; another to be told so openly.

It would have helped, perhaps, if there had been something to dislike about Angelica, but her nature was as warm and friendly as her face, and Gina found herself attracted by her sunny character almost against her will. She was a good dancer, too, and although she worked hard, had the humility of all true artistes and did not push herself forward.

If we had met under different circumstances I should want to be her friend, Gina thought. *Certainly she is going to be a real asset to the Eastern.* But if she couldn't compete on the looks front, Gina experienced the dawning of a competitive spirit dance-wise, and toiled even harder than usual in class and rehearsals.

'Angelica's good for you,' Madame Berthe told her. 'You needed someone to spark off and pace yourself against.'

'So she's good for my professional if

not my private life,' Gina told her reflection, before forcing herself to her feet to get dressed.

She was still changing when Angelica popped her head around the door and asked if she could come in.

'Please do.' Gina smiled.

'I've a bit of a problem,' the other girl admitted. 'I've been looking for a flat in the city and can't find one anywhere. You haven't any ideas, have you?'

'A flat? Why — don't you like it at Melrose?'

'Of course, but it was always only a temporary arrangement. I came to spend one week, and have been there over a month now. Jude says I should stay, but I want a place of my own.'

Gina frowned. 'But I thought — '

'That he and I are an item?' Angelica finished the sentence for her. 'No — though people used to tell me he had a thing for me, we are just good friends, as they say. He's a real balletomane and knows lots of dancers.' She smiled conspiratorially. 'Actually, I've got a boyfriend, so staying at Melrose is cramping my style somewhat!'

Gina dismissed the glow of happiness that enveloped her as quickly as it came. *Steady on;* she told herself, *she might not love him, but he wants her — he as good as admitted that was why he became a partner in the Eastern — to impress her. He must know about Angelica's boyfriend and be using desperate measures to try and woo her away from him.*

'We could look in the newsagent's window down the road,' she suggested. 'Have you tried there? Just give me a minute and I'll be with you.'

They walked together to the shop, and as they looked in the window, the proprietor, Mr Patel, hurried out to talk to Gina.

'You gave in, then?' He sounded resentful. 'You finally sold out to the developers.'

'What are you talking about?' She was surprised by his antagonism. Usually the street was united in all its doings.

'The theatre — you've agreed to its demolition.'

She stared at him, taken aback by his words.

'We haven't agreed to anything of the sort. Where did you hear that we had?'

'It's in the local paper — come inside, and I'll show you.'

She followed him into the shop, where he opened the *Branchester News* and pointed to a small article at the bottom of a page. It described proposals for a new development on the site of the Little Theatre — and as she read the name of the company concerned, she understood. It was Relly Holdings.

'I'll kill him,' she muttered under her breath. 'I really will kill him!'

Now at last she knew the real reason why Jude had wanted the Eastern. To get his hands on their only asset — the site of the Little. Theatre. How naïve she had been to assume he had bought it for love — he might want Angelica, but he wanted money more. She remembered him telling her at Melrose that he had other plans for the offices of his new headquarters — no wonder he had not mentioned where he meant!

And Stan — how had he been involved? Could it be that Jude had employed the stagehand to foment trouble at the theatre? If the proposed strike had gone ahead, the company would have lost thousands of pounds and been forced to sell. Stan must have been the alternative arrangement in case Jude was unable to persuade James to let him become a partner — the so-called sacking having been put on for her benefit once James had invited Jude to take over and the stagehand was no longer needed.

'Don't worry, Mr Patel,' she said, sounding more confident than she felt, 'leave this to me. There's obviously been a mistake, and I intend to sort it out.'

She left Angelica copying out an address from an advertisement in the window, and ran back to the theatre.

'Mr Alexander has gone home,' the

girl in the box office told her, and Gina's shoulders slumped. How on earth could she reach him there? What she had to say could not be done over the phone.

'Do you want a lift, Gina?' Alicia Allen had heard the urgency in her voice. 'I'm visiting friends and can drop you off on the way, if you like.'

The journey was torture for Gina. Alicia chatted gaily all the way about her excitement at dancing in *Anna Karenina*, and praising all the changes Jude had brought to the company.

'And I'm so glad you are going to dance on the opening night.'

'Me?' Gina questioned. 'Alicia, you are the prima ballerina assoluta — '

' . . . who just happens to be going to her niece's wedding that weekend, so Jude very kindly agreed you could dance on the Saturday night.'

'But the part was choreographed for you.'

'My swan song, before I hand over to the Swan Princess.' Alicia turned her face from the road for a moment to smile at Gina. 'It will be wonderful to dance the part, but I have a feeling that you will make it uniquely your own.' She pulled up by the gates of Melrose House and let Gina out.

Gina crunched up the gravel drive, deep in thought. Why did everyone think Jude Alexander was so very wonderful when she knew him for the scheming fraudster he was — determined to smash their home theatre to the ground and replace it with a faceless office building? She wondered if it was too late to stop him — what was it he had said about making decisions on her father's behalf? No doubt that business brain of his had left nothing to chance — she would be prepared to wager he had arranged every detail so that the sale of the Little Theatre could not be reversed.

'Hello.'

She jumped as he stepped out from the hedge he had been pleaching, bill hook in hand, the dark hair on his arms glistening with beads of sweat from the exertion. He flexed his shoulders and swung one arm around in a circle.

'I'm seizing up,' he said with a droll smile.

'I want to talk to you!' She ignored the shivers the flexing of his muscles was sending down her spine, refusing to be deflected from her purpose. 'How could you plan to demolish the Little? All your talk about being attracted to the arts, when in reality the only thing that drives you is money! That's why you wanted to gain control of the Eastern, isn't it? So that you could build your precious office block!'

'I see you have already read the local paper.' He wiped his hands on a large handkerchief. 'I was hoping to tell you myself, but the right moment never arose.'

'I'll bet!' she sneered. 'How do you find the right moment to tell someone you're going to disband a company you originally said you were going to save?'

'Who said anything about disbanding the Eastern?'

'Oh, please, don't pretend!' His calm

attitude infuriated her. 'Without a home theatre there's no way we can survive for long.'

'There was no way you could have survived at all if I hadn't taken over — you'll admit that if you're truthful.'

'That's ridiculous! Mr Lindt had extended our credit — in fact he had even given us another loan — so he must have believed we were viable.'

He paused, as if weighing up how much to say. Then, 'Ah, yes, the second loan. Tell me, did Lindt ever ask you to sign anything concerning that?'

She shook her head slowly, a horrible tightness in her throat. With a sick feeling, even before he continued, she realised that Jude must have had a hand in it somewhere.

'No, I thought not. You see I guaranteed both loans after we went to the dinner-dance, and once I'd done that, he was not worried whether you defaulted or not. He knew that the bank would get its money back one way or another.'

'You devious beast!' She recognised she had lost then, but at least she could tell him what she thought of him. 'So you had two back-up plans in case you couldn't manage to gain control by becoming a partner — you demand repayment of the loans or get Stan to call a strike and ruin us!'

He eyed her up and own, a stony expression on his face.

'You really don't know much about finance, do you, Gina? As a guarantor I would have no right to demand payment from you, though the bank could insist I paid them. And as for Stan — what you think I have to do with him, I can't imagine.'

'I'm sure he was planted at the Little to cause trouble.'

'Granted, but not by me. I wasn't the only one interested in developing the theatre, you know.'

'Are you saying he was employed by someone else?' She was just waiting for him to lie so that she could catch him out.

'Yes, and he admitted as much when I finally got the proof and tacked him on the subject. He didn't like being an informant, and was very furtive when I challenged him, but he told me how he'd been hired to come and make as much trouble as possible at the theatre in the hope that your father would sell cheaply.'

She remembered Stan's shifty attitude when she had seen them together in the city, and knew Jude was telling the truth.

'The developer had obtained a number of sites around the Little, but needed to buy the theatre before he could build. Your father had refused to sell on many occasions. Stan was his last hope.'

'So how come you now own them all?'

'Well, the theatre was the lynchpin to the whole development, and since I had access to that, I was able to convince the developer it would be sensible to let me buy him out. Stan's confessions came later, and purely served to confirm my earlier suspicions that the builder was not a very scrupulous man.'

Whoever owned it did not change the final outcome, she thought disconsolately.

'I think I would have preferred to have been cheated by a stranger than by someone I once trusted,' she said in a wobbly voice.

His face drained of colour and he swallowed hard.

'Come with me to the house,' he said. 'There's something I want you to see.'

Indoors he took her to his study, a modern refuge out of place in the Tudor mansion. Stark office furniture and state-of-the-art computerised equipment clashed loudly with the warm wooden panelling.

'Here.' He pointed to a table on which stood an architectural model of the new development. She wanted to feign indifference to the whole enterprise, but was curious in spite of herself. She leaned forward as he indicated the salient features.

'The row of houses here will stay,' he explained, and as he spoke his enthusiasm broke through, 'but we'll renovate them thoroughly to prevent further deterioration. We'll take part of their back gardens to build on, and demolish the shops that are here at the moment.' He pointed to show where he meant. 'They're beyond redemption and were never very attractive anyway, so will be no loss.'

'What about the people who earn their living there?'

'They'll all be offered premises in the new shopping mall at reasonable rents, no problem.'

'And the Little?' Her voice was tight.

'That comes down, too, I'm afraid. It's no use getting sentimental about it — it's a very inconvenient theatre.'

'Very inconvenient for your development!' She threw the accusation at him and studied the small model to see what would take its place. Sure enough, it was an imposing office block, built in the classical style, with an impressive pillared entrance hall.

'Let me show you inside.' He lifted out the top floors.

The layout looked vaguely familiar, and she frowned. Those large unfurnished rooms with wooden floors and rails running round three walls — she swung her head round to give him a puzzled look.

'Yes,' he said, 'ballet studios. And look, there are the showers, the changing-rooms, wardrobe department, property room . . . ' His face was half wary, half excited. 'And here's the theatre, below.'

She caught her breath as he removed another two floors to reveal a modern, highly equipped auditorium and stage. The architect had done his homework well, and no detail, however small, had been overlooked.

'It does away with all that hectic to-ing and fro-ing between Boundary Road and the Little. Do you like it?'

His voice brought her down to earth again.

'It's beautiful, but who is it for?'

'The Eastern, of course.'

By which he meant Angelica, she knew. He wanted the company to win her over, and boyfriend or no, she was bound to be impressed by this.

'That, as much as anything, is why we have to go on tour.' His reasoned explanation made sense now. 'We won't have a home base for at least two years, though we'll do limited seasons at Melrose.'

'Can the Eastern afford the lease on all this?' She waved her had towards the proposed school and theatre.

'Relly Holdings are paying a very good price for the site.'

'That wasn't what I asked you.'

He forced his hands into his pockets and strode over to stare out of the window. 'There won't be anything to pay. I'm giving the company the lease.'

Such generosity — he must be smitten, she thought, and all at once she realised there could be no place for her in the reformed company. Her body was too painfully aware of his love for another for her to stay around. She could not stand the heartache of watching him chase and win Angelica.

'I'm sure Angelica will be delighted — '

'Why on earth should I care what she'll be?' he railed at her with unexpected anger. 'For heaven's sake, Gina, what I want to know is what *you* think about it.'

'It's very nice — '

'Nice? Nice? That's damning with faint praise! Will you enjoy dancing there, do you think?'

'I won't be dancing there, Jude, I'm going away.'

His face froze and he held his body rigidly. Only his narrowed eyes and compressed white lips warned that a volcano was about to explode.

'Why?' The expected tirade did not materialise, and he sounded — what? Confused? Disappointed?

Suddenly the fight went out of her. Why bother to pretend? He was not the type of man to be easily put off, and would see through any lies she might proffer to explain her departure. And as she had decided to go, there was no longer any reason to keep her feelings secret — she had only needed to hide them when seeing him every day threatened her equilibrium.

'Because I'm in love with you. Oh, I know you love Angelica and probably find my feelings ridiculous, but there you are. That's why I can't stay — it would be too difficult for both of us to try and act naturally, knowing I feel the way I do.'

He crossed the room in two of his long strides, and tenderly took her face in his hands. He looked down at her, as if her expression was more reliable than her words.

She had not expected this silent third degree — she had thought he might turn from her in embarrassed silence, or pour himself a stiff drink from the cut glass decanter on the corner table — but had never imagined she would be subjected to such detailed scrutiny.

'Do you mean that?'

Again, that uncertainty.

'Yes — silly, isn't it? I can't think how I let it happen — '

'Cut it out, Gina — for once in your life!'

She turned to blink away a tear, determined he should not see.

'Don't worry, I won't break down and sob all over you. I know you don't love me.'

'Not love you?' He slipped his arms around her. 'What on earth do you think I've done all this for?'

'F-for Angelica.'

'Oh, you little fool!' But there was affection in the way he said it. 'Is that really what you thought? It seems we have been at cross purposes, but maybe this will convince you.'

He drew her closely to him, and feeling her hesitation, stopped to stare into her eyes.

'Just so there's no misunderstanding, I did it for you, Gina, and I love you very much, my dearest Swan Princess.'

She blinked. She could hardly believe

what she was hearing, but one look at his serious face convinced her.

Now at last she knew she need not hold back, did not have to keep herself in reserve, and she responded eagerly to his embrace.

'Darling girl,' he breathed into her hair, 'my own sweet Anna.'

'Anna?' She stiffened. Was he still thinking of Angelica?

'*Anna Karenina*,' he explained. 'That's when I fell in love with you — at the première of that fateful ballet.'

'You were there?' Disbelief and disappointment flooded her. She would have given anything for him not to have witnessed her failure.

'Yes. It was when I first arrived in Branchester, and being a ballet fan, I was eager to see the new James George ballet. As I watched you on stage in the first scene with Anthony May, so radiant and so technically perfect, I knew I had to possess you. I could see you had a great talent, but had yet to reach maturity as a person and as a dancer to give a truly rounded performance. I felt I could teach you that.'

'But *Karenina* was such a disaster — '

'David was a disaster, not *Karenina*, and certainly not you. Once he came on stage the whole atmosphere changed, and I hated him for what he was doing to you. Your tortured expression as you tried to salvage what you could tore at my heart, and I determined that somehow, I'd make it up to you. That's why I'm reviving the ballet, to prove to you it was not your fault. I spoke to your father, and told him that with you and a different partner, the ballet would be a sure-fire success.'

Gina cast her mind back to the conversation she had overheard on the terrace at Boundary Road. So Jude had not been angling for a partnership in the company then — merely discussing a new production of *Karenina*. She had got it all wrong.

Round-eyed, she said, 'Why didn't you tell me how you felt?'

'I was going to try and engineer a

meeting with you, but then I heard David was your fiancé. I couldn't believe you could love such a jerk, but rumour had it that in spite of the general belief that your parting was by mutual consent, when he went off to America you were in fact devastated, so I decided to bide my time to give you a chance to get over him.'

'Oh, Jude, I never really loved him!'

'Yes, I thought as much when you responded so ardently to my kiss. Having seen the sterile pas de deux between you two during the love scene in *Karenina*, then experienced your warmth myself, I felt sure David had not been the man for you.' His eyes blazed as his gaze held hers. 'You are such a passionate woman, you could not have held back with someone you truly loved. That was what made me dare to hope that you might return my feelings — but when you accused me of using you to reach your father, well, I despaired.'

'I'm sorry, I was an idiot.'

'Hush!' He gave her a long, lingering kiss.

'You didn't need to do all this for me, you know,' she said when he finally freed her. 'I love the Eastern, but I love you more.'

He gave her a tender smile.

'I know that now, but then I had to find an excuse to meet you and spend time with you, and joining the company seemed the best way. I came to as many of your performances as I could, but then Mr Lindt arranged for us to go to the dinner-dance, and I thought I had the problem licked. I fondly imagined I'd sweep you off your feet!'

She gave a soft laugh. 'I know the feeling well. I suppose we'd better tell Dad. He will be surprised.'

'Actually, I don't think he will. You see, I knew David pretended to love you to gain a position of importance at the Eastern and I didn't want your father to think that I was doing the same. So soon after we met, I went and laid my cards on the table — told him I loved you and that was why I had originally wanted to be a partner in the company.'

'That must have surprised him!'

'Not at all. He's a shrewd old bird, is James. He did warn me David's treatment had left you with a huge inferiority complex, and it would take a long time for you to believe in love again.' His arms tightened around her. 'I realised how astute he was when you turned against me after he had suffered his stroke.'

'I'm so sorry,' she said again.

'I forgive you now, but there were times when I could have wrung your neck! Every day you imagined some new conspiracy I was supposed to have plotted, and as fast as I proved my innocence of one charge, you'd dream up another!'

It was true, and she blushed at the memory.

'I asked James if he thought you had some ulterior motive for wanting the Eastern — I see now he gave me a very evasive answer.'

'Good! I hardly think it would have been appropriate for your father to break the news to you! He knows about the demolition of the Little, by the way — I would never have gone ahead with my plans without his blessing — and he agrees to all my proposals ... so, do you?'

She nodded, eyes shining.

'Yes, now that I understand, I do.'

'We'll buy the ring tomorrow, then.' Seeing her stunned expression he added, 'Well, you said you agreed to all my proposals. I take it that you will marry me, won't you?'

Her smile was wide and unmistakable.

'Oh, yes please, Jude, there's nothing I'd like better in the whole world!'

We do hope that you have enjoyed reading this large print book.

Did you know that all of our titles are available for purchase?

We publish a wide range of high quality large print books including:
Romances, Mysteries, Classics
General Fiction
Non Fiction and Westerns

Special interest titles available in large print are:
The Little Oxford Dictionary
Music Book, Song Book
Hymn Book, Service Book

Also available from us courtesy of Oxford University Press:
Young Readers' Dictionary
(large print edition)
Young Readers' Thesaurus
(large print edition)

For further information or a free brochure, please contact us at:
Ulverscroft Large Print Books Ltd.,
The Green, Bradgate Road, Anstey,
Leicester, LE7 7FU, England.
Tel: (00 44) 0116 236 4325
Fax: (00 44) 0116 234 0205